ESCAPE TO THE FARM ON MUDDYPUDDLE LANE

Heart-warming, uplifting romance

Etti Summers

CHAPTER ONE

Nikki Warring closed her laptop and clapped her hands.

'Settle down, people. I'm not going to let you go until I have silence. Morgan, what did I just say?' She glared at the eight-year-old boy and mimed zipping her lips up.

The child scowled, staring at her from under lowered brows. But at least he had stopped talking. Finally. He hadn't shut up all day. Mind you, the rest of the class had been just as loud and unruly, trying to see how much they could get away with.

Because Nikki was a supply teacher and not their regular one, they wrongly assumed that she was fair game.

It was the same no matter which school she taught in, but after ten years in the classroom, all of them spent flitting from school to school, she was adept at reading a class and more than capable of keeping her charges under control.

It was wearing though and it did get a little tiresome, so she was mightily relieved that it was half term next week and she could have a well-earned rest. She was also looking forward to spending time with Sammy.

Nikki's heart clenched as she thought of her son, and she hoped he'd had a good day in school. However, the good days had become less and less frequent since he had started secondary school, and she dreaded the thought of him being upset again.

'Morgan,' she warned, seeing the child lean towards the girl sitting next to him. Nikki had already moved him twice today because he had been disruptive, and if he carried on she was tempted to have a word with whichever adult came to collect him.

The bell went and she dismissed the class, deciding not to bother. If she had been the child's regular teacher, she probably would have, but parents and carers tended to pay far less attention to supply staff.

Nikki quickly collected her things and hurried out, calling goodbye to the lady in reception. She was familiar with the school, having taught there on a number of occasions, and she guessed she would be back sooner or later.

Usually she was one of the first to leave a school when the bell went – not having any duties to delay her departure, unlike other members of staff – but on the last day of term there was always a scrum for the exit, no matter which school she happened to be in.

Getting caught up in a queue to leave the carpark, Nikki tapped her fingers impatiently on the steering wheel, anxious to be on her way. She never managed to arrive home before Sammy, but she was rarely long behind him.

The journey across Birmingham to their little terraced house in Bournville took about thirty minutes, the traffic being worse than usual because it was a bank holiday Friday, and she was hot, grumpy and tired by the time she pulled up alongside the house.

She paused for a moment, then took a deep breath and clambered out, hauling her handbag and resources bag, which also contained her laptop and looked more like a piece of carry-on luggage, with her.

The front door was unlocked, even though she kept nagging Sammy to lock it behind him as soon as he came home, and she shook her head in exasperation.

'Sammy?'

Dropping her bags at the foot of the stairs, she slung her jacket over the newel post. Sammy's school blazer had been cast aside on the bottom step, so she picked it up and hung that up also.

Nikki expected to find her son in the kitchen with his head in the fridge as he hoovered up anything remotely edible. Sammy was like a dustbin.

But to her surprise, the kitchen was empty and she checked the time. By her estimation, Sammy had only been home five minutes, so he should still be stuffing his face with the snacks she had prepared for him this morning before she'd left for work.

Unease stirred in her stomach.

'Sammy? Are you in your room?' she shouted.

No answer.

Wrinkling her brow in concern, Nikki went to the foot of the stairs.

'Sammy?' she called again.

A noise reached her, and although it was faint, she instantly knew what it was. Sammy was crying.

Nikki hastened upstairs and knocked on her son's door. 'Sammy?'

'Go away.' His voice was thick with tears.

No way was she going anywhere. He mightn't realise it, but he needed her. 'No can do. I'm coming in, okay?'

He didn't reply, so she gently pushed the door open and went inside.

Her son was on his bed, crammed into the corner, his knees up to his chest and his arms wrapped around his legs.

Her heart squeezed with pain when she saw his young face. It was streaked with tears, his eyes red, his cheeks blotchy, and his mouth was downturned.

He sniffed loudly.

Nikki sat on his bed. She desperately wanted to gather him to her and cuddle his hurt away, but she knew it was best to let him come to her in his own time.

'Do you want to tell me about it?' she asked, her voice soft. She could guess what had happened – Blake Fraser had bullied him again.

Sammy shook his head and sniffed once more, rubbing his arm across his nose.

Automatically Nikki reached into her trouser pocket and pulled out a tissue. 'Here. Blow your nose.'

Sammy did as she asked.

She tried again. 'What did Blake do this time?' It was telling that she had added 'this time.'

Her son refused to look at her so, taking a deep breath, she let it go – for now. When he had calmed down a bit, she would ask him again.

Anger tried to push its way to the surface, but she swallowed it down. Now wasn't the time nor the place. She would reserve her fury for when she spoke to her son's school. **Again.**

How many times had she contacted them to complain about Blake's treatment of her son? Ten? Eleven? But nothing was ever done, and it made her blood boil.

As a teacher she was aware of how difficult it could be to prevent and deal with bullying, but as a parent she wanted something done about it.

It had begun when Sammy transferred from primary school to high school last September. It was just little things at first, such as name-calling or taking his ruler and refusing to give it back. But over the two terms he had been there, the bullying had gradually escalated, and her son had gone from a child who liked school to one who was terrified of it.

Enough! She wasn't prepared to put up with this anymore.

It was too late to do anything today, and next week was the May half-term holiday, but as soon as school resumed, she would sort this out once and for all.

Sammy's sniffles were tapering off and he was looking at her miserably out of the corner of his eye.

Wordlessly she held her arms out and he scooted into them. As he cuddled into her, she held him as tightly as she could and kissed the top of his head.

'Shall we treat ourselves to pizza for tea?' she suggested when he pulled away. 'Then after we've eaten, we can start packing. I think both of us could do with a holiday, don't you? I bet you're looking forward to seeing Aunty Dulcie.'

So was Nikki. Not only was it a good idea for Sammy to have a change of scenery for a few days, but Nikki also couldn't wait to see her sister – or the farm she had recently won.

The lucky cow!

'Does Aunty Dulcie really live on a farm now?' Sammy asked his mother doubtfully.

Nikki glanced across at him and smiled, before quickly returning her attention to the unfamiliar road.

'She does! Isn't it exciting?' Nikki was incredibly envious, even though she had been sceptical when she'd first heard the news, as she had been convinced it was a scam. Win an actual farm? Hardly!

However, it had been totally above board and legal, and Dulcie had gone from renting a tiny flat in one of the less salubrious parts of Birmingham, to being the proud, if somewhat baffled owner of a farm on the outskirts of a quaint-sounding village called Picklewick. And the farm itself was on a road called Muddypuddle Lane. How cute was that!

Nikki couldn't wait to see Dulcie and have a proper catch-up. Video messaging simply wasn't the same as seeing her sister face-to-face.

Green fields lay on either side of the road, and Nikki could see rolling hills in the distance. She wound the window down to let in some warm late-May air, and breathed deeply, thankful that the journey hadn't been a particularly trying one. The traffic had been relatively light (considering that today was the start of the bank holiday weekend), the weather was gorgeous, and Sammy seemed to be coming out of his shell a little, even going as far as to seat-dance to a song or two on the radio. The shell was a recent thing; he had been building it gradually, layer by layer, since last September, each instance of bullying adding another coating.

It was with relief that Niki saw the shadows in his eyes lessen as they grew nearer to their destination, and his gorgeous smile reappear.

'Look! There's the sign for Picklewick!' Nikki exclaimed. 'We're almost there.'

'Can I play with the chickens?' Sammy asked. He had been thrilled to hear that Dulcie was the proud (although **proud** mightn't be strictly accurate) owner of three speckly brown hens.

Sammy was fascinated by the photos of them that his aunt had sent, and he had asked Nikki an extraordinary array of questions, most of which she hadn't been able to answer.

'I'm not sure whether chickens actually play,' she told him, hoping he wasn't expecting them to play fetch or chase sticks.

'Can I play with the cat?' he asked.

Nikki pulled a face. 'Aunty Dulcie says that Puss isn't very friendly.' Dulcie had used stronger language than that, when she had told her that the miserable so-and-so had ungratefully scratched her when she had tried to stroke it.

'Do eggs come out of a chicken's bottom, like poo?' Sammy asked, his thoughts leaping around like a frog on a lily pad.

'Er...Oh, look, isn't this lovely?' Nikki tried to divert her son's attention from chickens' bottoms to the pretty street they were driving along.

Artisan shops flanked either side of the road, and she spied an old square-turreted church and a whitewashed pub. She wondered if the food there was any good: Dulcie wasn't the best cook in the world and if Nikki wanted edible meals she suspected she would have to cook them herself, or they could eat out.

She came to a stop at a zebra crossing and smiled widely. Picklewick was gorgeous. Dulcie's photos hadn't done the village justice, and Nikki couldn't wait to have a mooch around in the shops.

The last person had crossed the road and as Dulcie waited for the lights to change, she noticed a police car on the opposite side of it. The officer was smiling at her and, worried that she had done something wrong and that he was about to pull her over, she began to panic. Until, that is, she realised she had been grinning like an idiot and he must have thought she was smiling at **him**.

The lights finally changed and the traffic began to move.

When she drew abreast of the police car, Dulcie glanced into it, and catching his eye, she smiled again and was relieved to see the man smile back.

The brief glimpse was sufficient to tell her that he was rather good-looking. Or was she just a sucker for a man in a uniform...?

'Down girl,' she muttered.

'Who are you talking to, Mum?' Sammy piped up.

'I'm practising what I'll say to the chickens,' she improvised, with a giggle that was most unlike her.

Ooh, this week at the farm was going to be so much fun!

Giovanni Alfonso loved Picklewick. There were a number of pretty villages on his patch, but he thought this one was the prettiest. Mind you, he was probably biased because he'd just bought a house here – and he had Megan to thank for that.

He would give her a call in a bit, to see how she was getting on. He didn't feel the need to check in on her so often these days. She had Nathan now, and although Gio would always be there for her, he didn't worry about her quite as much.

Those first months after Jeremy had passed away had seen Gio obsessively checking up on her, twice and sometimes three times a day. He owed it to the man – Jeremy had been a good mate as well as a colleague, despite the ten-year age gap. And he still missed the daft bugger; even after three years he called frequently to make sure Jeremy's widow was okay.

Gio decided to take a quick break and pop into the cafe for take-out coffee, after which he would give Megan a call.

As he sat at the pedestrian crossing waiting for the lights to change, a woman driving a silver Nissan waiting on the other side of the road caught his eye. She was smiling at him, and her grin was infectious, so he couldn't help but smile back. Then he wondered if he had misread the situation and her smile had been for someone else, because when she caught him staring, her face fell.

But as the lights changed and he drove slowly past her, he noticed that she was looking at him again, and this time her smile was definitely aimed at him.

Attractive, he thought, as he returned the smile once more. Guessing her to be in her early thirties, she had lovely twinkly eyes and a generous mouth.

Then she was gone, and he snapped his attention back to the road ahead as he searched for a place to park.

After he had bought his coffee and returned to the car, he sipped the hot liquid and phoned Megan.

'Hiya, it's Fonzo,' he said. 'How are you keeping?'

'Fonzo! Hi! I'm good. **Really** good. You?'

'I'm fine. Just thought I'd touch base and make sure you're okay.'

Her voice softened. 'I'm more than okay.'

'Nathan treating you right?' he asked. 'Because if he's not...'

'Don't go all macho on me, Fonzo,' she warned, but he could hear the warmth in her voice.

'I'm a police officer, I'm supposed to be macho,' he joked.

'Don't let any female officers hear you say that. What are you doing over the bank holiday? Are you working?'

'Actually, I've got a week off.'

'A whole week?'

He slurped his coffee. 'Yep. A whole week. Go me!'

'Does that mean you're free on Monday?'

'Not necessarily,' he replied cautiously, wondering what she had in mind and not willing to commit to anything until he knew.

'Have you got a **date**?' she cried. 'Good for you!'

'Er... no, no date.'

'What, then?'

Jeremy used to tell him how tenacious his wife was, and Giovanni knew she would get the truth out of him eventually. He didn't want to lie to her, and there was only so much evasive action he could take. 'Nothing,' he admitted.

'Fantastic! That means you'll be able to come to the show,' she said.

'What show?'

'The one Petra is putting on at the stables. It's not just a gymkhana, there will be loads going on. Oh, please say you'll come! We haven't seen you in ages.'

He noticed how naturally she referred to her and Nathan as **we**, and it warmed his heart. She had been utterly devastated by Jeremy's death, and Giovanni had despaired of her finding love again. He was delighted to see how happy she now was.

With a resigned sigh he said, 'Fine, I'll come. What time?'

'It starts at eleven o'clock. I'll be there all day, manning the cake stall. Shall I save you a slice?'

'Only one?' He allowed disappointment to creep into his voice. Megan's baking had always been legendary, but since Jeremy died she had started making cakes professionally and her business was taking off.

'Okay, two slices, but no more. Since you joined Traffic, you've been sitting on your backside all day.'

'Cheeky!'

'Gotta run, I've got a cake that's about to go ping. See you on Monday. Love you, Fonz.'

'Love you, too,' he replied, laughing. He meant it: Megan was like the older sister he'd never had.

He finished his coffee, clicked his seatbelt in, and was about to start the engine when a text came through.

It was from Megan, and he chuckled as he read it.

Bring a girlfriend, indeed! Megan knew damned well that he didn't have a girlfriend, because if he had, Megan would be the first to know about it.

Unbidden, a pair of twinkly smiling eyes swam into his head, and he thought of the woman driving the silver Nissan.

Yeah, right, as if that was ever going to happen.

With a wry shake of his head, Giovanni
went back to work.

CHAPTER TWO

Nikki wandered into her sister's kitchen on Monday morning, rubbing her bleary eyes and yawning. 'Have you seen Sammy?'

Dulcie was standing at the sink, her hands in a bowl of soapy water. 'Good morning, sleepy head. Or should I say, good afternoon? He's outside somewhere. With the chickens, I expect.'

'It's not that late, is it?'

'It's half-past ten. Can I make you some breakfast?'

'Just coffee, thanks.' Nikki slumped into a chair and yawned. 'I'm not used to late nights anymore.' She winced as she remembered how much wine she and Dulcie had drunk last night. They'd had a wonderful catch-up session and had chatted for hours.

They hadn't had a chance to spend time together alone on Saturday evening because Dulcie had been eager to show Otto off to her. He had cooked them the most scrumptious meal she had ever tasted, and afterwards Nikki had sprawled on the sofa in a food coma before the excitement of the day had caught up with her and she had taken herself off to bed.

Yesterday had been spent exploring the farm and, as Nikki had suspected might happen, Dulcie had roped her into doing a few chores.

She had baulked at cleaning out the chicken coop, though. Ugh! But Sammy had been well up for it, to her surprise, and she'd teased him about it, saying that she expected the same degree of enthusiasm the next time she asked him to tidy his bedroom.

Dulcie put a couple of steaming mugs on the table. 'Bees,' she said, brightly.

'Pardon?' Nikki scowled. How could Dulcie be so chirpy after all that wine? It wasn't fair.

'I've been thinking about keeping bees.'

'Why?'

'Diversification,' Dulcie said.

'Diversification from what?' Nikki blew on the scalding liquid before taking a sip.

'It's what farmers have to do these days.'

'You're not a farmer,' Nikki pointed out with a laugh.

'If I want to keep this place, I'm going to have to do something with it. And I like honey.'

Nikki's brow furrowed. 'I like wine, but I'm not about to grow grapes.'

'Hmm...there's an idea. Grapes.' Dulcie squinted as she thought.

'I love you to bits, Dulcie, but you can't keep a spider plant alive, let alone vines. You've definitely not got green fingers, and from what I can gather, vines are fussy and not very easy to cultivate.'

'Back to bees, then.' Dulcie beamed at her.

'Do you know the first thing about bees?'

'No, but I can learn. I didn't know anything about chickens until I got this place.'

Nikki sniggered as she remembered Otto's description of her sister's first encounter with a hen.

'Shut up,' Dulcie said. 'I know what you're thinking. I was surprised, that's all. I didn't expect there to be any hens.'

'Or sheep,' Nikki added. Otto had also shared the Flossie incident with her, and she'd almost split her sides laughing as Otto had recounted how his dad's tame sheep had chased Dulcie into the house and demanded to be let in because it wanted to be petted.

'That creature has got a hard head,' Dulcie protested.

'Bees sting,' Nikki pointed out.

'Only if they feel threatened. I've been looking into it.'

'I'm sure you'll work something out, and if keeping bees means that you stay afloat, then go for it.'

'Thanks, sis. I don't want to be a customer care advisor forever. I really want to make a go of this place.'

'I don't blame you for that. It's gorgeous.'

The farmhouse may be in need of renovation (seriously – that bathroom was a nightmare) but it had so much potential and Dulcie had already done a considerable amount of decorating, although there was some way to go yet and Nikki suspected she might be asked to wield a paintbrush before the week was over.

The grounds around the house – the garden, the veggie patch and the orchard – also could do with a large dose of TLC, and some of the fences needed to be repaired. The barns and the other outbuildings could do with some attention, and the fields surrounding the farmhouse had turned into meadows due to them not being grazed. They were currently full of late spring and early summer wildflowers, and Nikki smiled as she thought that the bees would be happy.

There was even a small stream tumbling down the hillside, forming little waterfalls and pools deep enough to paddle in.

It was absolutely idyllic.

She finished her coffee and got to her feet. 'I'll find Sammy and remind him that we are going to the show at the stables today,' she said.

Dulcie laughed. 'He hasn't forgotten. It was all he could talk about at breakfast.'

'Thanks for looking after him while I was lolling about in bed.'

'You obviously needed the sleep.' Dulcie gave her a meaningful look.

Nikki had shared her concerns about Sammy, and Dulcie appreciated just how stressed she was.

Thankfully, her son seemed to have come out of his shell a little since they'd arrived at Lilac Tree Farm, and the happy fun-loving boy that he had once been was starting to show his face again.

She knew that not having to go to school for a week had a great deal to do with his improved mood, but she also suspected that not being in Birmingham also helped. It was a fair-sized city, but there was always the prospect of bumping into Blake, and Nikki had an uneasy feeling that her son was continually on edge.

This little holiday to Lilac Tree Farm was already doing him the world of good, and he was throwing himself into rural life (the bit they'd seen of it) with enthusiasm.

Now, time to prise him away from those blasted chickens, before he started clucking like one.

As Gio drove up Muddypuddle Lane, he could see that there was a hive of activity at the stables. Jumps had been set up in one of the lower fields, and in another there were stalls and vans, and the aroma of doughnuts and onions was in the air. He was surprised at how many people had turned up, and it took him a while to locate Megan after he'd parked up.

The array of cakes on her stall was amazing.

'Did you bake all these yourself?' he asked, as he hugged her and gave her a kiss on each cheek, Italian-style.

'I did,' she confirmed. 'Although, this one here and that one—' she pointed to a couple of three-tiered wedding cakes '— aren't real cakes. They are fake ones for display purposes, and I use them to showcase my decorating skills, such as they are.'

'Stop being so modest. You've got a real talent. Jeremy would have been so proud of you.'

Megan glowed. 'He would have, wouldn't he?'

Not all that long ago, Megan would have teared up at Gio saying such a thing, but although there was a momentary flash of sadness in her eyes, it was swiftly replaced by quiet pride.

'Do you want to have a slice or two now, or would you like to take your cakes home with you?' She gestured to the cakes under their see-through domes.

'I'll take them home with me, if that's okay?' He chose a couple of slices – although making a decision wasn't easy because they all looked delicious – then he left her to it, as she was busy serving customers.

He was idly watching a load of kids clambering around on a fortress constructed out of bales of straw and remembering the days when he used to love doing stuff like that, when he felt someone clap him on the back and turned to see who it was.

'Nathan, my man! How goes it?' he cried. Gio gave Megan's other half a quick once over.

The guy was looking good. Older than Megan by a couple of years, Nathan's hair was peppered with grey and he had crow's feet around his eyes. Wiry and strong, he was the stable manager, and spent most of his day wrangling horses and tractors. At least, that's what Megan said: Giovanni assumed there was a bit more to the guy's job than that.

'Fancy a pint?' Nathan asked. 'We've got a beer tent, although it's less tent and more gazebo.'

Giovanni felt honoured. Nathan was normally taciturn and definitely not a people-person, so Megan must be having a good influence on him.

'I'm driving, but I'll have a glass of something cold and non-alcoholic.' Gio narrowed his eyes at Nathan in mock displeasure. 'How are **you** getting home?

Not driving, I hope?' Nathan didn't live at the stables; like Gio, he and Megan lived in Picklewick. Megan had sold the house she had lived in with Jeremy, Nathan had sold his tiny cottage, and they had bought a house together in the village – one with a decent-sized kitchen so Megan had room to bake her cakes.

'You coppers are never off duty, are you?' Nathan chuckled. 'Don't worry, Megan is driving. Anyway, I'm only having one. Come on, I've got something I want to ask you.'

'Ask away,' Giovanni said as soon as they were seated at a table, their drinks in front of them. The white plastic chair wasn't the most pleasant thing he'd ever sat on, and he shifted around to get more comfortable.

'You've known Megan a long time,' Nathan began. 'How do you think she'll react if I ask her to marry me?'

Gio was taken aback. 'Um, I'm not sure. How long have you two been an item?'

'Since a year last January. I never imagined I'd want to marry again, but this feels right, you know?'

Actually, Giovanni didn't know.

He'd had more than his fair share of relationships over the years, but he had never once felt serious enough about a woman to contemplate marriage.

'Do you love her?' he asked.

'She's my world.' Nathan's reply was heartfelt and direct.

'Does she love you?' Giovanni thought she did, but Megan had never said as much to him.

'She does.' Nathan sounded certain.

'I can't say for sure how she'll react,' Giovanni said. 'All you can do is ask her.'

'What if she says no? It might spoil everything.'

'What if she says yes?' he countered.

Giovanni didn't envy Nathan's predicament. What he **did** envy was the love Nathan shared with Megan, and he wondered whether he would ever get to experience that for himself.

He supposed he would have to meet someone for that to happen, but he was too wedded to his job. Shift work and unpredictable hours made it hard on relationships, which was why so many of his colleagues were divorced or separated.

He was better off not going down that road, he told himself, not for the first time. If he ever did meet a woman he felt serious about, he would cross that bridge when he came to it. For now, he was happy enough on his own.

Okay, not **happy**: contented.

Are you sure about that? his subconscious muttered in his ear, and at that very second he could have sworn he spotted a familiar face. A woman's face that brought a smile to his lips, an echo of the smile he had given her the other day.

But a gang of teenagers passed in front of him, and when he looked again the driver of the silver Nissan was nowhere in sight.

'Mind if I join you?' Harry, Petra's husband lowered himself into a chair. He had a pint in his hand and he took a deep draught, then smacked his lips. 'Ah, that's better. Don't tell Petra. She thinks I've popped back to the house to check on the baby. Lena and Amos are looking after him,' he added, seeing Nathan's raised eyebrows. 'He's fine. I gave Amos a quick ring to check. He's having a nap. The baby, that is, not Amos. They'll bring him down later.' He turned his attention to Giovanni. 'Fonzo, isn't it? Megan's friend?'

'And Nathan's,' Gio said. He gave Nathan an almost imperceptible nod. Nathan nodded back, and Giovanni knew his message had been received and understood. The friendship came with the proviso that Nathan didn't hurt Megan. Megan had been hurt enough.

'Petra is looking for you,' a male voice said, and Gio glanced up to see Otto York, Picklewick's celebrity chef, walking towards them. He was holding hands with a woman, and another was with them.

Giovanni was unprepared for the sudden blast of attraction when he saw who it was.

The woman noticed him at the same time, and her eyes widened.

'Please don't tell her you found me,' Harry begged, gesturing to his half-drunk pint.

'We won't. We thought we'd have a quick one ourselves. I don't know about Dulcie and Nikki, but I could murder a pint.

Dulcie, what would you like?' He turned to the woman whose hand he was holding.

'I think a nice cold glass of cider would go down a treat. What do you say, Nikki?'

Giovanni had a name for her. **Nikki.**

Now that he could get a good look at her, she was even lovelier than he'd first thought. Her eyes were conker-brown, and unlike the other day when her hair was back off her face, it hung loosely about her shoulders in chestnut waves. The two women had similar features, although Dulcie's hair was darker, and he guessed they were probably related. Sisters, maybe?

'Sammy, would you like a drink?' Otto asked, and Nathan noticed a boy of around ten or eleven, hovering shyly behind her.

Nikki's son, he thought, remembering catching a glimpse of a kid in the passenger seat of her car. He hadn't taken a great deal of notice though, too caught up in staring at Nikki herself.

'Anyone else want a refill?' Otto asked, sweeping a glance at the three men. 'No? Okay. Sammy, do you want to come to the bar to help me carry them?' The boy nodded and the pair headed to the bar.

Harry grabbed a couple of chairs from a nearby table, and he, Nathan and Gio shuffled around to make room for the women to sit down.

Gio had assumed that Nathan and Harry knew both women, so he was surprised when Dulcie introduced Nikki to them.

'Harry is Petra's husband – remember me telling you about her? Petra owns the stables – and Nathan is the general manager. I'm sorry, I don't know your name…' Dulcie said to Gio.

'Fonzo. I'm a friend of Nathan's.'

'Hi, I'm Dulcie, and this is my sister, Nikki. The hunky guy at the bar is Otto, and the boy with him is Sammy, Nikki's son.'

'Hunky guy?' Harry scoffed, good-naturedly. He pulled a face, then leant towards Giovanni and said in a stage whisper, 'Not only is he a handsome fella, he's a bloody good cook too. A Michelin star chef, apparently. Of course, his head's almost too big to fit through his front door.'

Dulcie threw a beer mat at Harry, and he ducked.

However, Gio wasn't taking a great deal of notice of the banter. He was more interested in watching Nikki. She had an indulgent expression on her face, but her gaze kept slipping away to the bar, and whenever it landed on her son, worry shadowed her eyes.

He glanced at the boy, wondering why she was concerned about him, but he couldn't see anything obvious.

Otto and Sammy returned with the drinks, and Giovanni sat back, letting the others do the talking.

He noticed that Nikki didn't say much either, and her son was positively mute. Then again, why would a kid his age be interested in grown-up chatter? The boy's attention was on the various activities going on beyond the gazebo.

Giovanni's might have been too, if it wasn't for the fact that he was struggling to take his eyes off Nikki. He didn't know why, but she fascinated him.

'I'm going to take a look at that stall selling Mexican food,' Otto said, finishing his drink in record time, and Gio refocused on the conversation.

'Anywhere there is food is a busman's holiday for you,' Dulcie joked. 'I'll come with you – you can treat me to an enchilada, or something. Nikki, are you coming?'

'You go ahead, I haven't finished my drink yet.'

'Aw...' Sammy pulled a face at his mother.

'Don't tell me you're hungry?' Nikki asked, her eyebrows raised in mock disbelief.

The boy's eyes lit up and he nodded.

'Okay, then.' She picked up her cider, but before she could drink it, Dulcie made a suggestion. 'You stay here. Sammy can come with us, if you like?'

'If you don't mind?' Nikki said doubtfully.

'Why should I mind? I don't get to see as much of this little guy as I'd like. Let me spoil him.' Dulcie beamed at the boy, who grinned back.

'Alright.' Nikki subsided, and Giovanni felt a spike of pleasure that she wasn't leaving just yet.

However, Harry and Nathan were, fear of Petra's wrath making them hastily swallow the last of their pints.

'Better make a move before Petra sends out a search party,' Nathan said. 'It's alright for you, Harry, she can't sack **you**.'

'She can make my life a misery, though,' Harry grumbled, upending his glass and tipping the dregs into his mouth.

'Fair point,' Nathan conceded. 'See you, Fonzo. Nice meeting you, Nikki.'

Then they were gone, leaving Gio and Nikki alone. And for what was possibly the first time in his adult life, Giovanni was tongue-tied.

The police officer hasn't got a lot to say, Nikki thought, wondering how to breach the awkward silence after the others had left, and she wished she had gone with them. To give herself a second or two grace, she drank a mouthful of cider, and as she swallowed she caught him looking at her.

'I'm not driving,' she said, feeling instantly guilty, even though she hadn't done anything she shouldn't have.

'I'm off duty.' His voice was deep and slightly gruff. It sent a shiver down her back.

Damn, he was hot.

Did she just think he was **hot**? Hells bells, how old was she? She sounded like Maisie. That was the kind of thing her youngest sister would say. At twenty-four, Maisie was the baby of the family. She acted like one, too.

'Are coppers ever off duty?' she shot back.

He chuckled. Another shiver, this time felt right through her.

'Probably not,' he said. 'You know what I do for a living, so what do you do?'

'I'm a primary schoolteacher.'

'Do you enjoy it?'

'I love it. Most of the time. How about you?'

'I love being in the police force. Most of the time,' he added.

He smiled at her, and she smiled back. 'Fonzo? Is that short for anything?' she asked, scanning his face as he spoke.

'Alfonso.'

'Italian?'

'Got it in one.'

'First or last name?'

'Last.'

'What's the first?' she asked, enjoying the quick-fire banter.

'Giovanni.'

'Double Italian?'

'On my father's side and my mother's. What about you?'

'Double Birmingham.'

'You don't have much of an accent.'

'Neither do you,' she countered. 'Do you speak Italian?'

'Not a word. Do you speak Brummie?'

'I'm fluent.'

'Are you from around here?' he asked.

'No. Are you?'

'I live in Picklewick. Whereabouts do you live?'

'Is this a police interrogation?'

'This is a Fonzo interrogation.'

'Is that what people call you? Fonzo?'

He shrugged. 'It's easier to say than Alfonso.'

'What does your mother call you?'

He licked his lips, and she couldn't take her eyes off his mouth. 'Gio,' he said.

'Can I call you Gio? Fonzo sounds like a bear.'

'Are you referring to Fozzie Bear? I didn't think you were old enough to remember the Muppets.'

'They're still going strong, and if that's a subtle way of asking me how old I am, I'm thirty-five.'

'It wasn't, but thanks for the info. Are you here on holiday?'

'I suppose you could say that. I'm visiting my sister for a week. She owns Lilac Tree Farm.'

'I heard it had changed hands. It used to belong to Otto York's father, Walter.'

Nikki wondered if he knew the full story behind the change of ownership.

'Nice place,' he added.

'Do you know it?'

'I know of it, but I've never had any dealings with either Walter or the farm. I have been up to the stables a few times, though.'

Nikki raised an eyebrow, wondering whether it had been for work or pleasure. 'Riding?'

'Horse theft,' Gio explained. He glanced around, his eyes focusing on the world beyond the gazebo. 'Petra and Harry have done wonders with the place since I was here last.'

'I think Dulcie is planning on doing wonders with hers, but she's got a way to go yet. The house needs a complete makeover, and no doubt I'll get roped into helping while I'm here. She's already hinted that the bedrooms need decorating.'

'Sounds like it's not going to be much of a holiday. If you fancy a few hours off, how would you like to go out for a drink one evening?'

Nikki froze. Had Gio just asked her out on a date?

She wiped her suddenly damp palms on her jeans as unobtrusively as possible. 'Er...um...I can't. I've got Sammy, you see, and I can't leave him alone.'

'Who is leaving Sammy alone?' Dulcie asked, appearing at her elbow.

'I would be, if I went out for a drink with Gio,' Nikki told her.

'This **week**? While you're staying at the **farm**?' Dulcie asked. A slow, knowing smile was spreading across her face.

'Yes,' Nikki replied reluctantly. She had a feeling she knew what was coming.

'He won't be on his own, will he, you muppet. He'll be with me,' Dulcie said.

Nikki's eyes flew open, and she shot Gio a quick look.

'Muppet?' he mouthed, smirking.

Dulcie continued, 'Otto and I can babysit. It'll give me some practice.'

Nikki's eyes widened even further. 'Are you pregnant?'

'No. But one day I hope to be, and I don't get to see Sammy as much as I'd like, so I'll enjoy having him all to myself for an evening. I'll teach him how to play poker or something.'

'You wouldn't dare! Where is he, anyway?'

'Otto took him to see the show jumping. I hope you don't mind? I've only just got my head around chickens – horses are a step too far at the moment, and Otto is used to big smelly animals.'

'I don't mind,' Nikki said, trying not to. She wasn't keen on horses, either. Or cows. She was with her sister on that one, but Sammy was fascinated by any kind of animal. Look at the way he'd taken to the chickens! He had even tried to make friends with Puss, but the ginger tom hadn't been too keen and mostly kept out of Sammy's way.

'Seriously, we'll have fun,' Dulcie insisted. 'And the practice will do me good.'

Nikki knew how in love with Otto Dulcie was, and she felt a twinge of envy as she remembered when she used to be just as full of excitement for the future. These days she was considerably more jaded – getting married too young with a baby on the way, and a subsequent divorce, tended to do that to a person. She had only just completed her teacher training when Sammy had arrived, and not long after that, her husband of only a few months had disappeared out of their lives.

Gio was still waiting patiently for her answer, but Nikki continued to dither. Was going on a date with a man she had only just met and one who she was unlikely to see again after this week, a good idea?

She felt Dulcie's breath on her ear as her sister whispered, 'Go on, go out with him.

It's about time you let your hair down and had some fun. What harm can it do? You're hardly likely to see him again.'

'But that's the point,' Nikki retorted quietly.

'Huh. Do you look at every date as a potential husband or long-term relationship?'

'God no! I wouldn't want to put myself through that again. I'm fine on my own.'

'You might be, but that shouldn't stop you from having fun. It's even more of a reason to enjoy a fling while you can.'

Nikki batted Dulcie away with a strained smile. This was starting to get embarrassing. What must Gio be thinking?

'Sorry, Gio, just finalising a few details. I'd love to have a drink with you one night,' she said, suddenly making her mind up and hoping she wouldn't regret it.

And that was it – Nikki was going on a date with a man she didn't want to go out with, even though he was entertaining and seriously sexy, and all because her annoying sister had embarrassed her into it.

CHAPTER THREE

Going out for the evening was becoming
an increasingly pleasant prospect, Nikki
decided as her date with Gio loomed
larger. She hadn't been out in ages, often
too knackered to want to go anywhere in
the evenings, even during the school
holidays, although she did manage the
occasional lunch with friends. The
realisation that since she and Greg had
split up her world had gradually
narrowed, until all she did was look after
Sammy, go to work and do chores, was
an unsettling one.

What had happened to the formerly exuberant, outgoing, fun loving Nikki? She had been ground down by life's disappointments, all her fizz knocked out of her, that's what.

So it was with a gently bubbling sense of excitement and a smattering of nerves that she got ready for her date with Gio.

There was another reason for her keenness to go out this evening, and that was due to a growing suspicion Dulcie and Otto could do with some time alone, without feeling they had to entertain her. For all Dulcie's insistence that she wanted to spend time with her nephew, Nikki guessed Sammy wouldn't be long to bed. All this exercise and fresh air was wearing him out.

Nikki wasn't faring much better herself, and she hoped she would be able to keep her eyes open this evening. Despite pretending not to be enthused about helping Dulcie with her never-ending decorating, Nikki had thrown herself into it with enthusiasm. It was a welcome change from lesson preparation and herding pupils.

'You look lovely,' Dulcie said, when Nikki trotted downstairs in a pair of her sister's high heels. It was lucky they were the same size shoe-wise, although borrowing anything else belonging to Dulcie had been more problematic as Nikki's taste in going-out clothes was far more conservative than her sister's.

She hadn't thought to bring much in the way of smart clothes with her, not anticipating anything more than a meal or two in a local pub, so she was relieved to be able to team a floaty blouse (Dulcie's) with a pair of capri pants (her own). The high heels and a borrowed clutch bag completed the look.

'What time will you be back?' Sammy asked. He seemed a little apprehensive about her going out without him, and as she did it so rarely, she completely understood.

She wasn't going to allow her son to guilt-trip her into calling it off, though. Anticipation at the thought of seeing Gio again swirled through her. This was so unlike her, that it made her feel positively giddy. It didn't matter that nothing could ever come of it. She intended to enjoy this evening for what it was – a date with a handsome stranger.

In fact, it was refreshing not to have to worry about whether he would ask to see her again. She wouldn't be checking her phone every five minutes, or jumping out of her skin whenever it rang, hoping it might be him. A few drinks, some (hopefully) pleasant conversation, and maybe a kiss at the end of it: although she didn't want to think about that too closely, because the thought of his lips threatened to send her into a tailspin. That was all this would be, and if she was lucky it might be just the kick up the backside she needed in order to drag her non-existent social life out of the proverbial cupboard under the stairs, blow the dust and cobwebs off it, and take it out for a drive or two.

She wasn't referring to dating, as such, because she wasn't sure she could be bothered with the hassle, and she also had Sammy to think of, but maybe she could join her friends on a couple of nights out, even if it was only for a glass of Prosecco and some overpriced tapas.

'Your fella is here,' Dulcie said, cocking her head, and Nikki heard the noise of a vehicle pulling into the yard.

Her tummy fizzed with excitement and she stamped down on the unfamiliar feeling, not wanting either her sister or her son to see just how much she was looking forward to this.

'Say ta-ra to your mum, then you can help me put the chickens to bed,' Dulcie told Sammy.

'Where are you going?' Sammy asked, his eyes on Nikki.

'I'm not sure.' She shrugged nonchalantly. 'Just out for a drink in a pub somewhere.'

'Why can't I come?'

'Because, soft lad,' Dulcie said, steering him towards the back door, 'Your mum needs some grown-up time. Anyway, you'd be bored out of your skull.'

Nikki saw Sammy stifle a yawn, and she bit back a smile. She didn't think it would be long before he was in bed.

'See you later, Sammy. I'll tuck you in when I get back.'

He seemed satisfied with that, so she blew him a kiss and hurried outside.

Gio had got out of his car and was walking towards the house, but he drew to a halt when he saw her approach.

Nikki faltered, unsure of the correct procedure these days. She was fairly sure that shaking hands wasn't the done thing, but should she go in for a quick hug, a peck on the cheek, or what?

Gio solved her dilemma.

He stepped towards her, held out his arms and drew her to him.

A light touch, a swift kiss on each cheek, then he released her.

'I thought we could go to the Black Horse in the village,' he said, opening the car door for her.

Nikki unfroze her feet and got in. She was still reeling from the brief contact. During those few seconds, she had been close enough to get an enticing whiff of his aftershave and to feel the muscles in his back as she had quickly returned the embrace.

She had also felt a hint of stubble as her mouth brushed against his cheek, and now her lips were tingling.

The rest of her wasn't faring much better, and she realised just how long it was since a man had paid her any attention.

Nikki settled herself in the passenger seat, thinking what a novelty it was not to be the one driving. But she silently cautioned herself not to get carried away and have more than one drink.

'I thought you might feel more comfortable being nearer to the farm, considering you don't know me that well,' Gio said, breaking into her thoughts.

Nikki was touched by how considerate that was. 'I don't know you at all,' she countered with a smile.

'You know I'm a police officer and I live in Picklewick.'

'That's not much, is it?'

'It's a start.' He flashed her a glance as the car moved. 'What else would you like to know? Go ahead, ask me anything.'

'You might regret saying that.' She thought for a moment, as the car trundled down the hill. 'What's the most embarrassing thing you've ever done?'

He blinked, and she could tell that he had been expecting her to ask a more mundane question.

'Aw, this isn't happening,' he groaned theatrically. 'Ask me something else.'

'Uh-uh.' Nikki shook her head. 'It can't be that bad.'

He pulled out of Muddypuddle Lane and onto the road leading to the village, and sighed. 'I once told my girlfriend's mother that I loved her.'

'**What!?**' Nikki giggled.

'I was only seventeen. We were at her place. Her parents were out and we'd been getting all kissy-kissy. Nothing heavy, but she was my first proper girlfriend and I'd had a crush on her for ages. Anyway, she went to the kitchen to fetch a drink, and her parents came home. Neither of us heard them come in – I don't know if her mum was hoping to catch us doing something we shouldn't, but she was ever so quiet. I heard someone enter the living room and naturally assumed it was my girlfriend. I'd been trying to pluck up the courage to tell her I loved her for ages. I had my back to the door, and I remember staring at the tv and just saying it. I was so embarrassed, and her mum was horrified. So was my girlfriend. She broke up with me soon after. The whole school got to hear about it, and I didn't live it down for ages.'

'It's funny what stays with you, isn't it?' Nikki sympathised. 'I threw up in assembly once, and I still cringe when I think about it. It went all over the hair and down the back of the girl in front. Amanda Couler, her name was. I was called Barfie for weeks.'

'Barfie.' Gio sniggered.

'Don't,' she groaned. 'I wish I hadn't started this.'

'We're here,' he said, pulling into a car park behind the pub. 'We can swap more embarrassing stories inside.'

'Let's not,' she said. 'My worst one involves a year three child, a school inspector and lots of pooh.'

Gio wrinkled his nose as they walked towards the entrance. 'I might just be able to trounce you on the yucky stories,' he said, holding the door open for her.

'This is cosy.' Nikki gazed around in delight. This was exactly what she imagined a village pub should look like: inglenook fireplace, old beams, whitewashed stone walls. In fact, it reminded her of Dulcie's house.

'What can I get you?' Gio asked, and after they'd got their drinks they sat down, Nikki suddenly felt shy.

It didn't last long, though. To her relief Gio was incredibly easy to talk to, and the conversation flowed between them. She discovered that he was a year younger than her, had never been married, had always wanted to join the police force, and had parents who were still together and still in love. She also found out that he was an only child, that he pretended to like footie because all his mates did, and could knit – not that he did much of it.

In turn, Nikki told him about her ex-husband, skipping over the details of their divorce. She also told him she had a sister younger than Dulcie, and a brother in the middle. She shared her love of cooking, tv dramas, and hot water bottles.

He's a nice guy, she thought, halfway through the evening, feeling glad that

Dulcie had bulldozed her into going on a date with him.

Gio was the kind of man that she could fall for – if she was looking for a fella and if they didn't live so far apart.

But she **wasn't** looking, and they **did** live miles away from each other. And not only that, she fell for Greg, so that went to show what a crap judge of character she was. Trusting another man after her ex-husband was going to be hard.

Trusting her own judgement was going to be even harder.

If questioned, Gio couldn't explain why he had asked Nikki on a date, but something about her had spoken to him. And it wasn't just that he fancied her, although she was very pretty.

He could see her as a primary school teacher – calm, firm, yet with a softer side, and from the (often hilarious) stories she had told, he discovered that she had a wicked sense of humour and seemed to genuinely care about her pupils.

It might have been his imagination though, but he sensed she was worried and he guessed it was to do with her son. She clearly loved the boy with all her heart and her pride was evident, but something was bothering her.

'How is Sammy enjoying his holiday?' he asked.

She looked surprised that he wanted to know. 'It's doing him the world of good,' she began, then her expression clouded.

'Don't tell me, you're worried that he might want a chicken of his own?'

'I wish! That would be the least of my problems.'

Gio stayed silent. If she wanted to tell him she would, but he wasn't going to press her.

She ran a finger around the edge of her glass, her gaze distant. 'He's really unhappy at school,' she said, 'and it breaks my heart to see it.'

'He's in the first year in secondary school, you said? Is it because he has moved up from the primary?' Gio used to love his old primary school. He couldn't say the same about secondary, though. Too big, too many kids, too many tests. In primary he had felt cared about. In secondary he had soon learnt he had been just a number, and a fairly inconsequential one at that.

'Yes and no,' Nikki replied cryptically. She took a deep breath and let it out slowly. 'I think he would have been okay with the transition, if he wasn't being bullied.' Anger flashed in her eyes but quickly faded, replaced by worry once more as she continued, 'I came home from work on Friday to find him crying his eyes out.'

Gio's heart went out to the boy. He knew from experience how awful people could be to each other, but he was dismayed at how young some of them were.

'Isn't the school doing anything?' he asked.

'It doesn't seem like it. I've spoken to them several times, but nothing changes.' She looked towards the ceiling, blinked a couple of times, then dropped her gaze to him. 'Sorry, you don't need to hear me carping on about my problems. This is supposed to be a date. Let's change the subject.'

'I'm happy to talk about whatever you want,' he said, reaching across the table to put his hand over hers. 'If talking helps, we'll talk about it.'

'Thanks, Gio, but I don't want to think about it anymore tonight. There'll be time enough for that when we're back home next week.'

A tremor of disappointment at the thought of not seeing her again passed through him, and he willed himself not to be so silly. He knew before he had asked her out that this wasn't going to be the start of anything. It was just a pleasant drink with an attractive woman.

Respecting her wishes, he changed the subject, and she was soon laughing again, the rest of the evening passing on a lighter note.

'Thanks for a lovely evening,' Nikki said, as the car drew to a halt in the farmyard. It was eleven-fifteen, so not terribly late, and lights were on in the house.

'My pleasure,' Gio replied. 'I'm glad you enjoyed yourself. I had fun, too.'

Did he sound wistful?

Nikki shook herself. Unlikely. It was probably wishful thinking on her part; just because she was attracted to him and wouldn't have said no if he asked to see her again, she wanted him to feel the same way. But the distance scuppered any possibility of that happening, and both of them knew it.

There was a brief awkward silence as Nikki wondered whether he would kiss her, then she reached for the door handle.

'Nikki?'

She hesitated and looked at him. Her heart began to pound as he leant towards her.

But all he did was brush his lips against her cheek.

She closed her eyes, his mouth lingering, feeling his warm breath on her face, opening them again as he drew back.

'It was nice meeting you.' The formality of the words was lessened by a hint of regret in his voice. 'Take care of yourself, and I hope you sort things out for Sammy.'

She hoped so too, but right now her mind wasn't on her son. It was on a man who, under different circumstances, she could quite easily fall for.

Downhearted, she got out of the car, giving him a little wave as he drove off.

Then she braced herself for her sister's inevitable interrogation and went inside, pushing her melancholy to the back of her mind.

No use crying over what was never going to be. Gio was a pleasant highlight in a lovely week in the country. Nothing more.

CHAPTER FOUR

'With respect, Mrs Hardcastle, the school has had multiple opportunities to deal with this situation, yet the bullying continues. And it's getting worse. Do you intend to wait until some serious harm comes to my son before you take action?' Nikki demanded.

The headteacher's lips narrowed. 'We do not condone bullying in this school.'

'Yet, here we are. **Again.**' Nikki was trying hard to keep a lid on her anger, but this was the third time in as many weeks that she had sat across the table from this woman, and still nothing was being done.

Sammy was terrified and miserable, and it broke her heart to see him like that.

The headteacher continued, 'We've placed the two boys in different classes where we can, and where this isn't possible, they are seated apart. All staff members are aware of the situation, and all do their best to keep an eye on Sammy. But you must understand that there are nearly 1200 pupils in this school and—'

'I don't care about the other 1199,' Nikki broke in. 'At this point, the only child I care about is my own. His physical and mental health is suffering, and so is his academic progress, which I'm sure will be mentioned in his school report. But how can you expect a child who is scared out of his wits, to concentrate on algebra, or write a haiku poem?'

The headteacher drew in a slow breath and Nikki prepared herself for what she knew was coming.

'Maybe this school isn't the right one for Sammy?' Mrs Hardcastle suggested.

This conversation was one that Nikki had already played out in her mind. 'I was thinking the same thing myself,' she said, noticing with annoyance the relief in the woman's eyes. 'However,' she continued firmly, 'I don't see why my son, who is the victim here, don't forget, should be the one who is forced to move schools because another child repeatedly assaults him. Despite your gross lack of duty of care where Sammy is concerned, academically this is the best state school in the area. Besides, all his friends are here. If I took him out of here, away from his friends, I would, in effect, be punishing him, when it is the other child who should be punished.'

Mrs Hardcastle glared at her. 'What do you suggest, Mrs Warring? That we permanently exclude Blake?'

'Yes.'

'Pardon?'

'That is exactly what I am suggesting. There are three weeks left until the end of the academic year. That should be enough time to either permanently exclude him, or arrange for him to be moved to another school. Or do I have to put in a formal complaint to the Chair of Governors? Oh, and any future instances of assault will lead to me involving the police.' Nikki got to her feet. 'Thank you for your time, and I look forward to hearing from you in due course.'

And with that, she marched out of the meeting room, leaving the headteacher with a shocked expression on her face.

As Nikki walked through reception, she collected a distraught-looking Sammy, who had been waiting for her, and stamped across the car park.

Furious didn't begin to describe how she felt. Yet again, she had come home this afternoon to find Sammy cowering in his room, and when she saw the bruises blossoming on his thin arms, she had bundled him into the car and driven to his school. Once there, she had demanded to speak to the headteacher, and had informed the poor receptionist that she wouldn't leave the premises until she did.

Luckily, Mrs Hardcastle hadn't left for the day, although Nikki suspected that the woman would have refused to speak to her without an appointment.

Unfortunately for the headteacher though, at that very moment Nikki had seen her walking down the corridor, bag in hand. She was chatting to a colleague about looking forward to a quiet evening in front of the telly, so without the convenient excuse that she was in a meeting or that she was leaving to go to an appointment, the woman had no reason not to speak to Nikki.

Nikki wondered whether she had been too harsh, but she had meant what she'd said. She didn't want to transfer Sammy to a new school, because nothing about this situation was his fault. But she was serious about putting in a formal complaint and involving the police, if necessary.

But then again, what would all this do to Sammy? The formal complaint wouldn't affect him as such, because that would be held internally, but involving the police **would**.

They would want to speak to him at the very least, and she didn't know whether he was strong enough to cope with it.

Maybe it was for the best if she started to look for a new school for him after all.

This one might be the best school in the area, academically speaking, but Sammy was in no position to benefit from it, and she would much prefer him to be happy and settled, rather than worry about what grade he might get in any future examinations. The way he was going in his current school, he wouldn't do very well anyway.

Sammy was very quiet on the way home, and she kept shooting him worried glances. His face was pale, his eyes huge and shaded with purple. She knew he wasn't sleeping properly, his rest fitful and disturbed, and several nights he had woken from a nightmare, shaking and terrified, and it had taken her ages to settle him back to sleep.

Nicky didn't know how much longer this could go on.

When she got home, she sat him down on the sofa.

'I don't want to have to do this, but I will if the school doesn't do anything and you agree to it,' she began. 'How would you feel about not going back to that school in September?'

Sammy's eyes lit up and it was the most animated she had seen him since their visit to Dulcie's farm. 'I don't have to go to school?'

'That's not exactly what I meant,' Nikki said. 'You would still have to go to school, but what if we try to get you into another one? What do you say?'

His face fell. 'I don't want to go to another school. I don't want to go to **any** school. Not ever.'

'Sorry, Sammy, but you have to. It's the law.'

She wasn't being entirely accurate, because home-schooled children didn't. But she had to work. She had a mortgage to pay, and the bills, and she was struggling to get by on her salary as it was, without giving it up completely to live on benefits.

Nikki expected tears or anger, but all Sammy did was sit there, his eyes downcast, his face closed, and her heart broke that little bit more.

Later, as she recounted the conversation she'd had with the headteacher to Dulcie, she told her sister that she wasn't hopeful of a positive outcome.

'Bless his little cotton socks!' Dulcie cried. 'Can I do anything to help?'

'I wish you could, and thanks for offering, but we've just got to wait. And hope. He is adamant that he doesn't want to change schools, but he's also adamant that he doesn't want to stay in his current one.'

'As soon as the summer holidays start, why don't you come visit the farm again?' Dulcie suggested.

'What needs to be decorated?' Nikki asked, with a tolerant sigh.

'Nothing,' her sister replied innocently.

'Fibber. I am tempted though,' Nikki added. 'Even if you do get me painting anything that moves.'

'Please say you'll come,' her sister urged. 'It'll do Sammy good. He loved it last time. And—' she lowered her voice '—I've got more chickens.'

'How many more?' Nicki asked suspiciously.

'Another nine. Otto is getting through eggs like you wouldn't believe and I resent buying them when I've got enough space for hundreds of hens.'

Nikki smiled to herself. Was this the start of a chicken empire, she wondered. Dulcie had come a long way since her first few days on the farm if she was keeping more of them.

'How is Otto's cookbook coming along?' Nikki asked.

Dulcie laughed. 'I'm sick of eating flowers. It's got to the point where if someone sent me a bouquet, I'd probably put it in a salad. Otto is hoping to get it finished by the end of October. I suppose autumn is prime foraging season, what with all the berries, nuts and mushrooms, so he should have enough recipes by then to fill a book.'

'You sound happy,' Nikki observed.

'I am,' was Dulcie's simple reply. 'Anyway, back to the summer hols. Are you coming or not? I promise you won't have to paint anything.'

'But what about Mum and Maisie? Won't they want to come?' Nikki was well aware how hard work her mum and her sister could be, and although she loved them dearly, having them both there at the same time wouldn't make for a peaceful holiday.

'I doubt I'll be seeing them again before the autumn, so you can stay for the whole six weeks, if you want.'

Their mother and Maisie had paid Dulcie a visit back in May, but Nikki knew that her mum wasn't too keen on the great outdoors and Maisie had yet another new job and another new boyfriend to keep her occupied. Mum had had a fine old time boasting to her friends about what a fantastic place the farm was though, and how lucky Dulcie was.

Nikki made a decision. 'In that case, I'd love to come, thanks.'

'Yay! It'll be fun! Oh, and guess who I bumped into the other day? Fonzo! He asked after you.'

'He did?' Nikki's stomach turned over on hearing his name. 'That's nice of him,' she added, although she suspected he was just being polite.

Subconsciously, she touched her cheek, his kiss lingering in her mind. She had thought about him on and off since she'd got back; his face kept popping into her head at the most inopportune moments, and she would wonder whether he thought about her at all, believing it to be far more likely that he had forgotten she existed.

It was nice to think that he hadn't.

'How is he?' she asked.

'Good, I think. Still single.'

'Oh, no, you don't, Dulcie Fairfax,' Nikki warned. 'Just because you and Otto are all loved up, doesn't mean everyone else has to be.'

Dulcie chortled. 'You don't fool me. You like him.'

'What if I do? It doesn't mean I'm about to fall into bed with him, or fall in love.' Nikki's reply was firm. 'He's got his life and I've got mine. And there's also the fact that we hardly know each other. We've only been on one date!'

'Methinks, you doth protest too much.'

'If you don't stop trying to matchmake, Sammy and I won't come at all and you can look after your chickens all by yourself,' Nikki threatened.

She meant it, too. However nice the thought of seeing Gio again, there wasn't any point. She would just be teasing herself with thoughts of what could have been if circumstances were different. And that was assuming Gio was up for it, because she wasn't sure that he was, despite the connection she had felt between them.

But even though she knew she was right, a part of her hoped she wasn't.

Gio's thumb hovered over the screen for the second time that day, and for the second time he slipped the mobile phone back into his pocket.

He was supposed to be keeping an eye out for a car that was being driven on false number plates, but although he was parked up in a layby in an unmarked police vehicle, waiting for it to pass him, what he was actually doing was thinking about Nikki.

She had drifted in and out of his thoughts on a regular basis since their date, a pleasant memory of a lovely evening spent with a woman he had been very much attracted to, but since he had bumped into her sister yesterday he hadn't been able to get Nikki out of his head.

It didn't help matters that he'd had a message from Dulcie via Megan, that Dulcie wanted to speak to him, and could Megan pass on his number.

He was glad Megan had asked first, as he was quite particular who he gave his private number to.

His first thought when he had seen Megan's message was that something was wrong, either with Sammy or with Nikki herself, but Megan said she didn't think so, and was under the impression Dulcie wanted to speak to him about a social thing.

Gio took his phone out and read Megan's message yet again. A social thing could mean anything, but he had a sneaking suspicion it had something to do with Nikki, and he wasn't sure he was ready to go down that rabbit hole.

He'd had a great time and if things had been different he would have loved to see her again, but—

Damn. The car with the false plates just passed him.

Gio tossed his mobile onto the passenger seat and pulled out of the layby.

He had better stop thinking of what if, and concentrate on his job.

The false number plates turned out to be a false alarm, and after first dealing with an RTC, and then with a truck with a badly secured load, Gio found himself in Picklewick and heading to his favourite cafe. Relieved that the road traffic collision had been minor and that the truck driver hadn't given him any grief,

Gio wanted to get some food and caffeine inside him before he got another shout.

He had just left the vehicle and was stretching out the kinks in his back, when he spotted Dulcie. She noticed him at the same time and waved enthusiastically.

He was tempted to pretend he had an emergency and had to get back on the road PDQ, but that would be childish, so he stayed where he was.

Dulcie began talking as soon as she was close enough for him to hear what she was saying. 'Hi, Fonzo, I was hoping to speak to you. I asked Petra if she had your number, and she asked Megan, but I haven't heard back from her yet – but speaking in person is so much better, don't you think?'

'It depends on what's being spoken about,' he replied dryly,

Dulcie rolled her eyes. 'Nothing bad, obviously. Nikki is coming to stay with me for a few weeks in the summer holidays – Sammy too, of course – and I wondered if you'd like to pop up to the farm one evening for a meal? I've never held a dinner party, but Otto wants to try out some new recipes, and he was hoping for some fresh victims.'

From the way Dulcie was staring wide-eyed and earnestly at him, Gio guessed there was more to the story than she was letting on, and he had an inkling what that might be.

'Are you matchmaking?' he asked, and a blush crept into her cheeks.

'No...?' Her reply was hesitant, almost a question, which was why he didn't believe her. But he let it go.

He wasn't sure it was a good idea to go to the farm for a meal. He would be putting himself in a situation where the only logical outcome was that he would get hurt. He was a far cry from making a fool of himself where Nikki was concerned, but that was only because he had neither seen nor spoken to her since their date.

It was best if it stayed that way, because he had a feeling that she was a woman he could easily lose his heart to.

So he had no idea why he said, 'Sounds great,' and proceeded to give Dulcie his number.

Then he spent the rest of the day wondering how he could get out of it.

CHAPTER FIVE

As soon as she entered the farmhouse Nikki eased her trainers off with a sigh of relief and wiggled her aching toes. It wasn't only her toes that were aching; her calf and thigh muscles were too, and she eyed Sammy with resentment. Despite the long walk they'd been on, he was still fizzing around like a can of pop that had been shaken to within an inch of its life. Where did he get his energy from, and please could she have some of it!

All Nikki wanted to do was collapse onto the settee and not move for at least a week.

'Fancy a cuppa?' Dulcie called from the kitchen, as Nikki hobbled into the utility room.

'I'd love one.'

Dulcie stuck her head around the door. 'I was about to ask if you'd had a good time, but you look knackered. How far did you go?'

Nikki went into the downstairs loo to wash her hands, leaving the door open. 'Up to the top. We found an old disused cottage or barn. Sammy had a whale of a time poking around in it, making up stories of who might have lived there. The favourite seems to be a knight who was hiding out from a wicked king. Oh, and there was a wizard and a dragon in there somewhere.' She followed Dulcie into the kitchen. 'Hi, Otto.' She glanced around, noticing all the cooking activity. 'Are you practising a recipe?'

She dropped into a chair with a groan and rubbed her ankles. Bed was calling to her already, but with the best will in the world, five o'clock in the afternoon was a little early.

Otto shot Dulcie a look, and Dulcie smiled sheepishly.

Nikki's radar jolted into action. 'What?' she asked suspiciously.

'You haven't told her?' Otto tutted, shaking his head at Dulcie. He didn't seem particularly bothered though, so it couldn't be too bad.

'Told me what?' Nikki asked.

'Um, we're having someone to dinner.' Dulcie chewed her bottom lip.

Nikki guessed what the problem was. 'Do you want me and Sammy to make ourselves scarce? It's no problem, we'll go into Picklewick and grab something in the Black Horse.'

Driving into the village was the last thing she wanted to do, but it wasn't like she was only here for a couple of days. Dulcie had persuaded her to stay for at least four out of the six weeks that the kids were off school, and she was conscious that Dulcie mightn't want to entertain her all day, every day. In fact, it was Dulcie who had suggested that she and Sammy explore the hills above the farm this afternoon, and Nikki had got the feeling Dulcie had wanted her and Sammy out of her hair for a couple of hours.

Now she knew why: they were expecting visitors.

'You're eating with us, too,' Dulcie informed her. 'Do you honestly think Otto would cook a meal in my kitchen and not invite you to share it?'

Nikki shrugged. 'I wouldn't mind.'

'I know – you're the best sister ever.'

Nikki's radar pinged again. It had been finely honed by years of being able to tell when children were up to no good. And Dulcie was definitely up to no good. It was written all over her face.

Narrowing her eyes, Nikki asked, 'Are you going to tell me what's going on?' She had a feeling she wasn't going to like it. 'Who is coming to dinner?'

'Um...Fonzo?' Dulcie lowered her head and peeped up at Nikki from under her lashes.

'Stop trying to look cute and innocent. It might work on Otto, but it won't work on me.'

'I warned you,' Otto said to Dulcie. 'You should have told her sooner.'

Nikki sat up straighter. 'When you say **sooner**, when exactly did you plan this?'

'Acouplaweeksago,' Dulcie mumbled.

'Did you say **a couple of weeks**?'

'Oh, look, is that the time? I'd better...er...start getting ready.' Dulcie made a dash for the door, but Nikki caught hold of her arm.

'What time are you expecting him?' she demanded.

'Seven.'

'It's not even five-thirty yet,' Nikki pointed out. 'Why don't you stay and chat for a bit? Then you can explain why you invited Gio for dinner two whole weeks ago and didn't think to mention it until now!'

Gio mopped up the remaining sauce on his plate with some sourdough bread. 'Otto, that was amazing,' he said. 'You ought to set up on your own.'

'It might be most chef's dream, but not mine,' Otto said. 'As long as I have creative control in a kitchen, I'm happy. The last thing I want is to have to worry about the accounts, insurance, staff issues, and so on.'

Dulcie said, 'Fonzo is right – you should think about opening your own place. You're such a brilliant chef.'

Otto rolled his eyes. 'Yes, you can have some more if you want, but only if you leave enough room for pudding.'

'Ha ha. I've always got room for pudding.' Dulcie patted her tummy with a laugh.

Gio glanced at Nikki. She had been subdued all evening, and he hoped nothing was wrong. Sammy seemed perky enough, though, so whatever it was, Gio didn't think her son was the cause.

She looked up from her plate to find him staring, and Gio offered her a small apologetic smile. From the moment he'd arrived he had the impression that she wasn't keen on him being there. Although she had been friendly, he sensed a reservation in her that hadn't been there the last time he'd seen her.

The pleasure he felt when she smiled back, took him by surprise.

He hadn't been convinced that seeing Nikki again was such a good idea, and sitting at the table with her this evening had increased his reservations.

However, that one smile sent him into a tizzy, and he found himself thinking that he would do anything to keep that smile on her face.

Aw, damn it! This was precisely what he feared might happen. He was getting involved, despite knowing he might end up being hurt.

He should never have asked her on a date in the first place. If he hadn't, Dulcie wouldn't have invited him to dinner. Then again, he was a sucker for punishment because he could easily have said no: no one had forced him to come here tonight.

But he had wanted to see Nikki again, and that was where the problem lay.

He should have walked away, because no good would come of this.

Inhaling slowly, he wanted to kick himself. He had been around the block enough times to know it wasn't wise to start something he couldn't finish. It wouldn't be because he didn't want to – it would be because it was impractical and unworkable.

It was no good trying to tell himself to go with the flow and just enjoy it for what it was. He wasn't interested in a casual fling, and he got the impression Nikki wasn't either. Been there, done that, got the notch on his bedpost; but that was when he had been young, reckless and carefree, and when thoughts of settling down had given him the heebie-jeebies.

He'd grown up since then. These days falling in love was an appealing prospect, and the thought of spending the rest of his life with one woman was a gift, not a curse. He wanted what Nathan had with Megan, what Harry had with Petra, and if the soppy look in Otto's eyes was any indication, what the chef had with Dulcie.

But the problem was, Gio didn't want to fall in love when the woman he gave his heart to lived so far away.

He almost snorted into his pudding! He'd only had one date with Nikki, yet here he was worrying about getting his heart broken? If the poor woman had any idea what kind of thoughts had been going through his head just now, he wouldn't blame her if she jumped in her car and hightailed it back to Birmingham.

To say that he was getting ahead of himself, was the understatement of the year.

'Which is yours, Fonzo?' Dulcie asked.

Gio froze. 'Come again?'

Dulcie poked him in the shoulder and laughed. 'You were miles away. You didn't hear a word of that, did you?'

'No, sorry.'

'We were discussing ice cream. What's your favourite flavour?'

He replied without hesitation. 'Pistachio.'

'What did you think of this one?' Dulcie used her spoon to point at the remains of her dessert. There wasn't much left, only a dribble of pale purple creaminess.

'It was very nice,' he said. He had a vague recollection of eating it, but he couldn't for the life of him remember the details.

'Blueberry,' Otto said, 'with a hint of lemongrass.'

'Very nice,' Gio repeated, then made the mistake of glancing in Nikki's direction.

There was a twinkle in her eye and she was chewing her lip, and he could tell that she was holding back a laugh. His suspicion was confirmed when she leant across the table as Otto and Dulcie began the clean-up process after refusing any help.

'You were away with the fairies for a while, weren't you?' she said.

'Yeah, I suppose I was. Work stuff,' he added, unnecessarily.

'Nothing serious, I hope?'

'Nah. Just...things.'

'Things,' she repeated, deadpan.

'How about you?' His eyes shifted to Sammy, who had left the table and was heading towards the hall. 'Are things any better at school?'

'Worse, if anything,' she said, with a sigh.

'Why don't you two take the rest of the wine into the garden?' Dulcie suggested.

'We'll be out as soon as we've regained control of the kitchen. You would think a professional chef would make less of a mess. Fonzo, would you like a low-alcohol beer seeing as you're driving?'

'Please.'

Dulcie got one out of the fridge and opened it. 'Go on, shoo. You're making the place look untidy.'

Gio went outside, Nikki following, and they headed for a wooden table and benches in the middle of a scruffy lawn.

It was still light, although the sun had set and twilight was rapidly descending. Bats swooped and dived, chasing insects, and the air was warm and still.

As soon as they were seated, Nikki said, 'I think we're being set up. I'm sorry, I don't know what's got into my sister.'

'I don't mind. If I did, I wouldn't have agreed to come. I wanted to see you again.' He could kick himself. The words just slipped out, and he couldn't even blame it on too much beer.

'And I was thinking you were only here for the food,' she joked, but her expression was solemn.

'That, too. Otto's not a bad cook, is he?'

Nikki's mouth dropped open, then she realised he was being tongue-in-cheek. 'I hope this foraging cookbook works out for him,' she said.

'Do you think he'll go back to London?'

Nikki shrugged. 'I hope not, for my sister's sake. She's head over heels in love. But Dulcie tells me that his dad is getting better, so maybe he will.' She stared across the valley, the orange-streaked sky illuminating her face. 'She'll be devastated if he does.'

There! Right there. **That** was the reason he didn't want to start a relationship with a woman who lived so far away. Birmingham was hardly the other side of the Atlantic, but what with his shifts, weekend working and frequently long hours, combined with Nikki being restricted by the school day and term times, getting to see each other would prove difficult.

'It's so peaceful here,' she said after a while, the silence only broken by the whinny of a horse in the field below and the rumble of a distant engine. 'Dulcie is so lucky,' she added.

'Would you like to live somewhere like this?'

'I'd love to.'

'Wouldn't you miss the city?'

'I doubt it. Apart from travelling through it twice a day to get to and from work, I don't have an awful lot to do with it.' She leant forward, putting her elbow on the table and resting her chin in the palm of her hand. 'Sammy loves it here. He couldn't wait to come back, especially when he found out that Dulcie had added to her flock of chickens.'

'She seems to have settled in well,' he observed. 'At least she's got over her fear of them.'

Nikki giggled, a sound that melted his heart. 'She has! She's still not keen on sheep, though. I don't think she'll turn into a shepherdess any time soon.'

'What about you? Could you see yourself herding sheep?'

'Not on your nelly! Herding a class of pupils is enough. A dog to round them up might come in handy, though.' Her shoulders sagged. 'Sammy would love a dog, but it simply isn't possible. Otto says he can borrow Peg, but it's not the same. Sammy was hoping that the farm's resident cat would be amenable but he's a right grumpy so-and-so. Do you have any pets?'

'No, although I'm with Sammy on this – I'd love a dog. But it wouldn't be fair on the pooch. I hardly work regular hours and I often have to work late if the situation calls for it.'

'You live in Picklewick, you said?'

'That's right. Just bought a house here.'

'Lucky you!'

Giovanni agreed: he was incredibly lucky. Picklewick was a gorgeous village in a lovely location. 'I don't suppose you hire your decorating services out, do you? My house could do with a lick of paint.'

'You must be joking! I keep trying to ignore Dulcie's hints. I thought I was supposed to be here for a holiday,' she added, laughing. She stood up. 'It's getting late. I'd better put Sammy to bed. If he doesn't get a full eight hours, he's as grumpy as anything.'

'I know how he feels,' Gio replied. 'I'm partial to my bed, too.'

Nikki shot him a look, one he found hard to interpret. 'Goodnight,' she said. 'I expect you'll be gone by the time I've persuaded my son to get into his pyjamas.'

That was a hint for him to leave, if ever he'd heard one. 'Nice seeing you again,' he replied mildly, disappointment pricking at him.

He watched her walk away, her hips swaying, and he picked up his bottle of beer, glared at it, then put it back on the table, untouched. He wanted a proper beer, not this alcohol-free stuff.

Dulcie wandered out to join him. 'Want another?' She gestured to his drink, and he grimaced without meaning to. 'Yeah, I know what you mean,' she said. 'If you fancy a proper drink, you could always stay the night.'

Gio blinked in surprise. 'I don't think your sister would appreciate bumping into a strange man on the landing in the wee small hours.'

Dulcie gave him a speculative look. 'Oh, I don't know...' she replied archly.

Gio did: he was pretty sure that Nikki wouldn't be happy. 'I'd better be off. Thanks for a lovely meal.'

'She won't be long. Sammy's not a baby – he can put himself to bed. She'll be back down in a minute.'

He wasn't so sure about that. He had a feeling Nikki might stay upstairs until he left. 'Thanks, but I need to get going. Early start in the morning.'

He was about to walk off, when Dulcie stopped him in his tracks.

'She's scared,' she said.

'Of what?'

'Love, relationships, being hurt again. Her ex-husband was a real shit.'

Gio slowly sat down again. 'I think I would like that beer now, if that's okay?'

'Coming right up.'

Whilst he waited for Dulcie to reappear with his drink, Gio took the opportunity to ask himself what on earth he thought he was doing.

He didn't have an answer – not one that made sense. All he knew was that he was thinking with his heart and not with his head. Nikki fascinated him: vulnerable, capable, sassy, sad, sparky, withdrawn...She was an enthralling mix wrapped up in a stunning package. He had never felt as drawn to a woman as he was to her.

He was still musing on his own stupidity when he saw his beer appear.

It wasn't in **Dulcie's** hand though. Nikki was walking towards him, and she was carrying two bottles.

'Shall we go for a stroll?' she asked, after handing him one of them and drinking deeply from the other.

The bottle was slick with beaded moisture and deliciously cold. He took it and wrapped his lips around the top, swigging back a couple of mouthfuls. The liquid slipped down his throat a treat, and he wiped his mouth with his fingers.

'If you like.'

She left her bottle on the table and began walking. He quickly finished his and popped his next to it, then followed her, his pulse quickening at the thought of being alone with her.

A yellow moon had risen above the hill behind them, the light from it just bright enough to see where they were putting their feet. Beyond the garden lay the orchard and they made their way over to the gate, the tree trunks ahead dark, the shadows between them even darker. Leaves rustled in the soft breeze and the scent of honeysuckle floated in the air.

Long grass brushed against the legs of his jeans, and he trailed a hand through the nodding seedheads, following her deeper into the orchard. Soon they were surrounded by trees, the boughs laden with ripening fruit.

'These are apples and pears,' she said. 'And I think I saw plums on one, but I'm not entirely sure.' She halted and gazed around. 'We've only taken a few steps, and it's like we're in the middle of nowhere.'

Gio remained silent, not wanting to disturb her pensive mood. Lights from the farmhouse windows glowed, leaves dancing across them so they seemed to flicker, and if he peered down the hill, he could see the stables, and further afield Picklewick twinkled in the distance. An occasional sweep of headlights indicated a road, and when he looked directly overhead, stars were emerging.

It was a magical evening.

He was acutely aware of her nearness, the light scent of her perfume, the faint outline of her profile, the rustling of her feet as she shifted position.

Gio wasn't sure whether it was the location, the atmosphere, the intimacy, or all three, but he so badly wanted to kiss her, to taste those full lips, to bury his fingers in her hair and run his hands over her curves.

Instead, he took a deep breath and tried to calm his thudding heart.

Every cell in his body tingled and he felt more alive than he had ever felt – and they hadn't even touched yet.

How would he cope if they did?

He had to find out.

When Nikki had realised that Gio hadn't left and was still in the garden, she had been surprised and more than a little pleased. When she had told him she had to put Sammy to bed (a lie, because Sammy was perfectly capable of putting himself to bed) she had given Gio an out.

He hadn't taken it. And Nikki wasn't sure whether that was because he wasn't interested in her, or because he **was**.

Dulcie had shoved a stubby brown bottle at her and had told her to take it out to him, and impulsively Nikki had grabbed one for herself, and then asked him if he'd wanted to go for a stroll.

The orchard was fast becoming her favourite place on the farm, and she had taken to coming here when she needed space to think. She could breathe amongst the gnarled trunks, fill her lungs with oxygen-rich air and empty her mind. And night-time was her favourite.

Nikki stared out across the valley, picking out pinpricks of light in the distance. The warmth of the day lingered in the air, and she breathed deeply, relishing the rich smell of soil and growing things. And Gio.

The scent of him was tantalisingly male, with undertones of wood and citrus, and he was standing near enough to touch, if she could only find the courage.

Then she discovered she didn't need to: he found it for her.

His eyes were on her, not the view. It felt incredibly intimate, like a virtual caress, the darkness heightening her awareness until her skin glowed as though he had stroked her face with a finger.

She turned slowly.

No longer side-by-side, they were now facing each other, and in a single fluid movement she was in his arms and his lips landed on hers.

Closing her eyes and opening her mouth, she gave herself up to the sensations swirling through her, living only in this moment, the rest of the world eclipsed as effectively as the sun obscured the moon.

He held her gently, yet she felt his strength, and she wrapped her arms around his neck, drawing him to her.

Gio kissed her softly, but she felt his hunger, and her tongue found his, deepening the kiss until all she was aware of was his mouth, his arms, his body pressed tightly against hers.

When the kiss ended, his lips sliding over hers until they drew apart, he kept hold of her and she him, not wanting to let go, wanting to keep the moment alive for a few seconds longer as they stared into each other's eyes, her pulse soaring, her heartbeat loud in her ears.

Eventually she broke the spell when she turned her head and rested her cheek against his shoulder, and he lowered his lips to her hair, brushing the top of her head. It was more intimate than any kiss, and her heart melted a little bit more.

She didn't know how long they stayed like that, wrapped in each other's arms, the night deepening and darkening around them, but she knew she didn't want it to end.

If only things were different, she could seriously fall for this man.

But as they began to walk slowly back to the house and he took her hand in his, Nikki realised it was actually too late.

She had already fallen...

CHAPTER SIX

'Sammy, I'm not sure you're allowed.' Nikki reached out to grab her son, but he was already darting across the yard towards a row of stables. Three of them were occupied, equine heads poking over the tops of their half-doors, ears flicking with curiosity.

She and Sammy had taken a walk into Picklewick earlier, and she had treated him to cake and a milkshake in one of the cafes. He had devoured his with enthusiasm, chattering continually, his lively animation a pleasure to see.

But for once, Nikki's attention hadn't been wholly on her son. Part of her had been hoping she might spot Gio, and her gaze had kept returning to the street and the cars trundling up and down it.

Last night lay heavily on her mind.

The kiss had been perfect: just the right balance of passion and tenderness. Afterwards, they had returned to the house in silence, pausing when they arrived at the back door. And without saying a word, he had kissed her again, this time a brief, gentle brush of the lips as he cupped her face in his hands. She remembered pushing her cheek into his palm, and then he'd left.

She had listened to his footsteps gradually fade, her hand lingering on the door handle, reluctant to go inside just yet.

When she had no longer been able to hear them, she had let out a slow sigh.

He was gone, and she imagined him striding down the hill, his long legs eating up the ground, knowing he would have to come back. That single beer meant that he'd had to walk home, leaving his car in the farmyard, so she would see him tomorrow.

But to her dismay, his car was gone by the time she got up this morning, and she felt cheated and strangely bereft, as though he had abandoned her.

The hope of bumping into him in the village wasn't the sole reason Nikki had suggested a stroll into Picklewick. Sammy had an abundance of excess energy to burn off, and she was too restless to potter around on the farm – but it had been part of it.

After a bit of retail therapy (she had bought a scented candle for herself and some modelling clay for Sammy) and a stop for refreshments, they had made their way back to Muddypuddle Lane, following a footpath which led from the village, through open fields, past the stables, and on up the hill towards the moorland beyond.

Nikki was hoping the walk would have taken the edge off Sammy's energy, but when they'd reached the stables, he had shot off at top speed, eager to see the horses.

'Sammy,' she called after him, but it was too late. He was already petting the nearest one and giggling.

'Its nose is all soft and hairy!' he cried. 'It tickles.'

'Her name is Mabel,' Petra said, emerging from a shed with a bridle slung over her shoulder. 'She's probably hoping you've got a treat for her.'

Sammy's eyes widened. 'What sort of treat?'

'She likes carrots and apples, and she's also partial to a banana.'

He turned to Nikki. 'Have you got a banana I can give her, Mum?'

'Not on me, no,' Nikki chuckled.

'Here, give her these.' Petra bought out a handful of brown pellets from her pocket.

'What are they?' Sammy asked, as Petra showed him the correct way to feed a horse.

'Pony nuts. No, keep your hand flat, or she might accidentally eat your fingers.'

'Sorry,' Nikki said after Mabel had crunched up her treat. 'He got away from me. Anything to do with animals, and he's there.'

'I don't blame him. I prefer animals to people, as a general rule. You know where you are with a horse or a dog. People...? Not so much.'

'Come on, Sammy, let's go. I'm sure Petra has got better things to do than entertain us.'

'You can stay, if you like,' Petra said with a shrug. 'It makes no odds to me. In fact, Sammy can help out if he wants.'

Sammy gasped. 'Can I, Mum? Please!'

Nikki wasn't sure she wanted to hang around the stables, but after seeing the pleading expression on her son's face, she agreed. After all, there wasn't anything else she needed to do, and being here meant she could avoid decorating for an hour or two longer. It was mean of her, she knew, but she wasn't in the mood for painting a wall.

'Have you ever been on a horse?' Petra asked Sammy.

He shook his head, his eyes wide.

'Would you like to?'

Biting his lip, he looked to his mother for reassurance.

Nikki nodded her permission.

'Yes, please,' he said.

'In that case, we'll get Mabel saddled up and you can have a ride. You've got to earn it first, though,' Petra warned. 'I'm going to introduce you to Gerald, the donkey. He's got to have his hooves trimmed, so I want you to help me put a halter on him, then you can lead him out of the stable and tie him up just there.' She pointed to a large circular piece of metal embedded in the wall. 'After that, we need to muck out the stall, because as sure as God made little green apples, he'll have had a pee and a poop in there.'

Nikki had just parked her backside on what she assumed must be a mounting block, hoping she wouldn't get roped in, when the mention of apples took her straight back to last night in the orchard. She tried to ignore the image of Gio with his head bent towards hers and the desire she had seen in his eyes, and concentrated on the orchard itself. Tidying that up was something she'd like to get her teeth into, she thought, rather than being stuck indoors, painting.

As she had said to Gio (she silently told herself to stop thinking about him), the trees were already full of small apples and unripe pears, and she could just imagine how it would look with the ground beneath them cleared of the scrubby bushes and the brambles that were threatening to choke the fruit trees.

It was going to be quite a task, and she wasn't sure she had the time or the skills to be able to do it. However, she would like to try, and it would be one less job for Dulcie to do around the farm. She ignored the voice in her head that told her so would painting one of the bedrooms.

Whilst she was deep in thought, Petra came to stand next to her. 'I hope I wasn't stepping out of bounds when I said Sammy could have a ride,' the woman began.

'Not at all,' Nikki assured her. 'I'm very grateful. It's extremely kind of you.'

'He's doing me a favour. Mucking out isn't my favourite job. I'd much prefer to chat with you.'

'Despite me being a mere human?'

Petra barked out a laugh. 'I tolerate some people better than others. You might not believe this, but since I met Harry, I've mellowed a lot. I used to be much worse than this.'

'In that case, and while you're in a chatty mood, can I pick your brains?'

'There's not that many to pick, but go ahead.'

'I know you're not a farmer as such, but can you give me any advice on how to go about clearing the orchard up at the farm? It's badly overgrown and the brambles are threatening to take over. Although, saying that, they've got loads of berries on them.'

'If I were you, I'd pick them before I cut them back. Or let Otto loose on them. I'm sure he could do something wonderful with them.'

'Blackberry ice cream,' Nikki murmured, remembering the mouth-watering meal she had eaten last night. The meal wasn't the only thing to make her mouth water though, as she thought of Gio.

'Sounds nice. Not that I'd ever make any. But if there was some on offer...?' Petra cocked an eyebrow.

Hmm...that was a thought, Nikki mused. Home-made ice cream in unusual flavours.

'Seriously,' Petra continued. 'What you need is a goat. Or two.'

'A goat?'

'Goats are the best things for clearing the land, and they'll fertilise it for you at the same time.'

Nikki wrinkled her nose. 'Where on earth would I get a goat from?'

'Leave it to me,' Petra said with a smirk. 'Just leave it to me!'

Gio walked slowly away from the scene of the accident, thanking god that no one had been seriously injured. Or worse.

He had lost count of the number of road traffic accidents he had attended over the years, and although he tried to maintain an emotional distance, it wasn't always easy. And this one had touched him more than others, despite there being only minor injuries.

Getting back in his car and leaving the clean-up to the tow truck companies and Highway Patrol, he snapped his seatbelt on and started the engine. Then he rested his head against the back of the seat and took a steadying breath.

The driver of one of the cars had had a very narrow escape indeed. An improperly secured load of metal poles had slid off the rear of a truck when it had suddenly braked. The driver of the car behind hadn't been able to avoid the poles as they smashed into the front of his car, and one of them had missed his chest by a hair's breadth. A centimetre more, and the man would be dead.

It wasn't the first time Gio had attended a similar accident and it wouldn't be the last, but this one had abruptly brought home to him how fragile and uncertain life could be. The man was roughly the same age as him, facially they were fairly similar, and both had dark hair and dark eyes.

After Gio had quickly checked with the paramedics that the driver's injuries weren't life-threatening or life-changing, he'd had the sudden thought that it could have been him in that car. But maybe he wouldn't have been as lucky.

It wasn't a sense of his own mortality that kept him sitting there: it was the realisation that there were still so many things he wanted to do in life.

A trite saying popped into his mind – live every day as though it was your last. The sentiment was admirable, but unachievable for the vast majority of people. Like him, they probably had to work for a living, would have chores to do, and a million things that wouldn't be on top of anyone's bucket list but nevertheless still had to be done.

But sitting in his car and staring at the mangled vehicles in front of him made Giovanni realise that he wasn't living life to the full. He was holding back in many ways, and what was at the forefront of his mind at this very moment was Nikki.

He wasn't sure who had kissed whom yesterday evening. Had he initiated it, or had she?

Did it matter?

He'd thoroughly enjoyed it. Heck, he'd more than enjoyed it, he had been blown away.

As he walked home last night, he had told himself that it was because of the ambience of the night...strolling through an orchard, under the stars, with the scent of flowers in the air and a beautiful woman at his side, had been enchanting.

But it wasn't because of that, as nice as it had been.

It was because of Nikki herself.

He'd been all set to leave once he'd thanked Dulcie for the meal, but something she'd said had made him stay.

And it was possibly one of the best decisions of his life, despite the very real possibility that he might get his heart broken.

Because it was high time he started living – **really** living – and he knew just what he needed to do to make that happen.

'Apparently, she's more of a diva than a princess,' Nikki told Dulcie, handing the animal's lead rope to her son, so he was now holding both goats. 'That's her name, Princess. And the other one is called Toffee. Isn't she the most gorgeous colour?'

Dulcie didn't look convinced. 'What did you say I'm supposed to be doing with them?'

Nikki had told her once, but her sister hadn't taken it in. Dulcie had been too busy trying to avoid the curious creatures, dancing out of the way whenever they came too close.

'You don't have to do anything,' Nikki repeated. 'Sammy will be looking after them: under my supervision, of course.'

'But what will happen when you go back home? Who will look after them then?'

'Hopefully they'll have done their job of clearing all the brambles and other weeds from the orchard, so they'll return to the stables. And you never know, you might take a shine to them.'

'Nope. Not gonna happen. They've got horns,' she added in a low hiss.

Nikki grinned. Did Dulcie think the goats could understand her? And if they could, that they hadn't realised they had horns?

'Here's the plan. Sammy will tie them up in a different part of the orchard every day. Petra said that if they aren't tethered Princess will probably escape, and even if she doesn't, they'll eat all the fruit they can reach. Then Sammy will bring them into the barn at night. I might need some help to get set it up, though.'

Dulcie seemed dazed. 'Goats,' she repeated.

'Petra reckons they'll do a much better job of clearing the ground than we could ourselves, and in far less time. Oh, and

I've been thinking about selling ice cream.'

'You're a teacher. Why do you want to sell ice cream?'

'Not **me**. You.'

Dulcie's brows lowered. 'I can't see me driving around the streets in a van, playing **Greensleeves** and asking people if they want a flake with that, can you?'

'Actually, you and Otto,' Nikki amended.

'Oh, I don't think Otto would—'

'I'm talking about selling ice cream from the farm!' Nikki broke in triumphantly. 'New, unusual flavours created by Otto, that people could buy tubs of to take home to eat.'

Dulcie looked stunned. 'Um...it's certainly something to consider.'

Nikki could see she wasn't convinced. 'It was just a thought,' she said, deflating quicker than a soggy soufflé. Oh, well, she said to herself, at least thinking about orchards, goats and ice cream had taken her mind off Gio for a while.

'Come on, Sammy, let's get Princess and Toffee settled,' she said.

Sammy walked towards the orchard, importantly leading both goats, and Nikkii was about to follow him, when she turned back to Dulcie. Another idea to help bring in some much-needed cash for the farm had bubbled to the surface, and she was just about to suggest that once the orchard was cleared it might be possible to open it up to the public so they could pick their own apples and pears, when a flash of yellow and blue caught her eye.

A police car was turning into the yard.

Nikki squinted at it, and her tummy did a slow roll as she recognised the officer behind the wheel.

'Gio,' she whispered, and her fingers went to her lips, remembering the taste of him and the feel of his mouth on hers.

His gaze was on her face as he pulled up, got out of the car and slammed the door, then strode purposefully towards her, his eyes never leaving hers.

'Ooh,' Dulcie murmured. 'Look at him.'

Nikki looked. She couldn't tear her gaze away as he rapidly covered the ground between them, and she licked her lips nervously. Was this a formal visit or a—

'Eek!' she cried as he swept her into his arms, the sound cut off as his mouth descended on hers.

She froze, then she was frantically kissing him back, ignoring her sister's incredulous stare and excited squeal.

When Gio finally put her down and she could catch her breath, Dulcie cried, 'Richard Gere, eat your heart out!'

Nikki blinked. 'Who?'

'From **An Officer and a Gentleman**? The film where...never mind.'

Gio stared at Dulcie, but he quickly turned his attention back to Nikki. 'I just had to,' he said, by way of an explanation. 'Sorry.'

'You don't look it,' Nikki retorted.

'I'm not really.'

Dulcie clapped, and Nikki and Gio shot her a look.

'I'm sure you've got things to do,' Nikki said to her sister.

'I don't think so.'

'**Yes, you have**,' Nikki hissed.

'Oh, yeah, right. I've...um...got to... er...' Dulcie grinned. 'Bye, Gio.'

He waved absently.

As soon as her sister was out of earshot, Nikki said, 'That was unexpected.'

'Nasty unexpected, or nice unexpected?'

'Couldn't you tell?'

He wrinkled his nose. 'Nice?' he guessed.

'Very nice.' She glanced in the direction of the orchard. 'I would prefer a bit of warning next time, though,' she said, adding, 'Sammy.'

Gio closed his eyes. When he opened them again, he looked contrite. 'Sorry, I didn't think. Where is he? He didn't see, did he?'

'He's in the orchard with a couple of goats. Long story.' She waved a hand in the air and shook her head. 'I'll tell you another time.'

'I'll hold you to that,' he said. 'Um...look, I'd love to see you again, but I understand if you don't want to. You've got Sammy to think about, and you live there, and I live here, and then there's my job and—'

'Yes,' she interrupted. 'I do want to see you again.'

The sudden pleasure on his face made her giggle.

'That's great!' he exclaimed, then there was a crackle from his radio and his face fell. 'Excuse me a sec.' He turned away. 'Go ahead,' she heard him say as he moved off a few paces. When he turned back to her, he said, 'I've got to go. Can I see you tonight?'

'I can ask Dulcie if she would babysit.'

'You can bring Sammy along.'

Nikki gave him a level look. 'Not yet.'

Probably not ever, she thought. This relationship would only ever be a short-term one, so there would be no need for Sammy to get to know him. As far as her son was concerned, Gio was a friend of Dulcie and Otto. Nothing more.

But even as she was thinking this, she wished it could be much, much more than what was essentially a mere holiday fling.

Gio tasted of hops, the beer he had recently drunk lingering on his lips as Nikki's tongue eagerly sought his.

Her arms were wrapped around his neck, pulling him into her, and she couldn't seem to get enough of him. He filled her senses so completely that nothing else mattered

'Excuse me,' a gruff male voice said, and Nikki was abruptly brought back to earth.

Feeling like a teenager caught necking behind the bike shed by one of her teachers, she muttered, 'Sorry,' as they shuffled to one side to allow an old gent to get to the pub's door.

'I think we'd better make a move,' she told Gio, feeling the heat of a blush sweep into her cheeks. Standing on the pavement outside the Black Horse in full view of everyone with her mouth clamped on Gio's, wasn't the most appropriate thing to do. But as soon as they had stepped outside, she hadn't been able to keep her hands off him.

To be fair, Gio had been just as eager, and he was now looking dazed and dishevelled, his hair sticking up at odd angles and his breathing ragged.

'I think we better had,' he agreed, his eyes shooting towards the pub's windows, his expression one of embarrassment, and she realised that it probably wasn't a good idea for the local copper to be seen snogging in the street.

Nikki giggled.

'What's so funny?' he asked, slipping a hand into hers as they began to walk along the high street. His fingers caressed the back of her hand, sending shivers of longing through her.

'Us. We're behaving like a couple of teenagers.' She leant into him as they strolled down the pavement, feeling the solidity of his shoulder against hers.

'I suppose we are,' he agreed. 'It's fun, though.'

It was, but she hoped Gio didn't just see her as a bit of fun, as nothing more than a summer fling and a fleeting romance. Yet she knew it couldn't be anything else.

She pushed the thought away, not wanting to think of the future. It wasn't as though she didn't know what she was doing, and she was aware of the risks she might be taking with her heart if she was silly enough to fall in love with him.

Ignoring the little voice cautioning her that she was halfway there already (how could she be when she had only known him five minutes, she reasoned) she let go of his hand and wrapped an arm around his waist.

He did the same, holding her close, and they continued on their way, pausing every so often to kiss.

'Are you sure you want to walk?' Gio asked. 'It's not too late to call for a taxi.'

'I want to,' she assured him. It had been her suggestion to walk to the farm from the pub in the first place, although she had immediately felt guilty when she realised it meant he would have to walk all the way back to Picklewick after he said goodbye. But he had insisted that he didn't mind, claiming that the exercise would do him good.

In Nikki's opinion, Gio looked as though he got plenty of exercise anyway. He hadn't got that flat hard stomach and muscular chest from sitting behind the wheel of a car all day, and she guessed he must work out.

It was rather romantic strolling back to the farm in the twilight, especially when it was imperative that they had to stop every once in a while to kiss and cuddle.

Nikki didn't want the evening to end, but she knew it had to. Even if she didn't have Sammy to consider, it was far too soon to hop into bed with Gio, however tempting the thought. And she was forced to admit that she **was** sorely tempted. There was something quite liberating about the insular nature of a summer fling, and she felt like Sandy in **Grease**: summer lovin' was indeed a blast, and it was happening much faster than she could have anticipated, but that was all right, wasn't it, because it would come to a natural end soon enough – a summer fling that didn't mean a thing.

However, she had the feeling this wouldn't be a sweet romance, not with the heat sparking between them, and the thought of getting passionate with Gio sent waves of desire cascading through her.

Down girl, she admonished, and tried to tell herself that sleeping with him wasn't inevitable, even though she suspected that it probably was. There was nothing to hold her back. They were single consenting adults, and as long as they were going into this with their eyes open, no one would get hurt.

Something had definitely begun and that something would definitely end, but in between there was nothing stopping them from sharing several long, hot, summer nights.

Being impulsive was a trait Gio thought he had grown out of, but clearly not, as his actions earlier today had illustrated.

But he couldn't bring himself to regret turning up at Lilac Tree Farm and kissing Nikki in front of her sister, and neither did he regret asking her out. The evening would have been lovely, even without any kissing. With it, it had been **wonderful**.

It still was, because they hadn't reached the farm yet, and he found he was dragging his feet, not wanting the night to end.

But eventually the lights of the farmhouse came into view, and he had to let her go.

He wanted a few more kisses before he did though, and when she melted into his arms as though she was meant to be there, he held her tightly as his mouth sought hers and he lost himself in her embrace.

'You do realise I'm going to have stubble rash on my face tomorrow,' she said when they broke apart for the final time. She was smiling, so he didn't think she was overly concerned about having a red chin.

'I'll shave closer next time,' he promised.

'No, I like it. Not the rash, the designer stubble.'

'It's not designer,' he protested. 'I can't help it if my beard grows fast and it's really dark. Blame my Italian heritage.'

'I think it's sexy,' she declared, stroking his face, her touch making every nerve ending zing with longing.

He would give anything to take her to bed right now and make slow glorious love to her, but although he was hopeful it might happen in the future, it certainly wasn't going to happen right now.

'When can I see you again?' he asked.

'I'm not sure. There's Sammy to consider. I don't want to keep dumping him on Dulcie.'

Gio was disappointed but he understood. Her son came first, and that was only to be expected. 'What if I let you have my shift pattern for the next two weeks? If you can work something out, great. If not...' He left the sentence hanging.

'I'm sure I'll think of something,' she said. 'Petra at the stables has kindly offered to give him a riding lesson or two in exchange for him helping out, so what with that and Dulcie commandeering him for farm duties, I'm sure I'll have some time to myself.'

'I hope so. And I honestly don't mind if you want to bring him with you – we can do something together, something he might enjoy.'

'I'll think about it,' she said. 'He loves being at the farm, but this is supposed to be a holiday, so I don't want him to spend all his time mucking out the chicken coop and herding goats.'

'How about we go for a picnic? Or to the zoo?'

'I suppose wild animals will make a change from farm animals,' she replied thoughtfully. 'It's ages since we've been to one.' She seemed to come to a decision. 'Okay, we'll go on your next day off, if you like? But I warn you, there'll be strictly no kissing or canoodling.'

'Agreed. Now, can I have one more kiss before I say goodnight?'

Nikki lifted her chin. 'You may,' she replied primly, but the way she kissed him back was anything but prim, and when she finally pushed him away and went inside, Gio was glad of the long walk home – he needed it to cool his not-inconsiderable ardour!

CHAPTER SEVEN

'Remember, no kissing,' Nikki hissed at Gio, as she walked around to the passenger side of his car after making sure Sammy had buckled in his seatbelt.

Gio fake-pouted. 'I haven't forgotten. I promise I won't hold your hand, either. Or even look at you, if you don't want me to.'

'You're being facetious.' She pulled a face at him over the car roof, before getting in.

He was still grinning when he started the engine and drove out of the farmyard. 'You okay in the back, mate?' he called, and Nikki glanced over her shoulder

Sammy beamed back at her. 'I think he is more than okay,' she replied, on her son's behalf. 'He hasn't stopped talking about this since he got up this morning.'

Nikki had been tempted to do the same herself – not because she was excited to be going to the zoo, but because she was excited to see Gio again. It had been a couple of days and she was surprised at how much she had missed him. She hadn't been able to get him out of her mind, and Dulcie had teased her mercilessly, saying that she was mooning over him like a love-sick calf.

Nikki had hotly refuted it, but even she had to admit that she had caught herself daydreaming, and on more than one occasion she had realised that she had a soppy smile on her face.

Dulcie had smirked and suggested that it might be better for Nikki and Gio to spend his day off doing something else, and had offered to look after Sammy. But Nikki wasn't ready to take that step: after all, she'd only known him for a few weeks, and they'd only been on two dates so far.

It was a tempting thought, though...

However, she wasn't entirely sure that allowing Sammy to spend time with him was a good idea, because she didn't want to risk her son becoming attached. But as long as Sammy viewed Gio in the same light that he viewed Otto, she didn't see the harm in it. It wasn't as though she was introducing Gio as her boyfriend. As far as Sammy was concerned, Gio was simply a friend who was accompanying them to the zoo.

The journey passed quickly, with Gio entertaining Sammy with stories of the funnier or stranger aspects of his job as a traffic cop.

Sammy was fascinated. 'How fast can your car go?' he asked.

'This one? I'm not sure, because this is my own car, but unmarked police cars can reach speeds of up to 155 miles per hour.'

'Wow! That's fast. How fast are we going now?'

'About sixty-seven.'

'Can you go faster?'

'Not a good idea, mate. I'm not on duty today, so I've got to stick to the speed limit, like everyone else.'

A flurry of questions later, and Sammy ended up with an offer from Gio to sit in his panda car the next time he was in the vicinity of the farm.

'Will I be able to put the siren on?' Sammy pleaded.

'Only if your Aunty Dulcie says it's okay,' Gio replied. 'We don't want to scare the animals.'

'Princess doesn't get scared,' Sammy informed him solemnly. 'Toffee might, but she's only one year old, so she's still quite young, but she'll take her lead from Princess. Princess is her mum,' he added.

Nikki bit back a grin: her son sounded just like Petra, repeating word for word what the stable's owner had told him.

'What about the chickens?' she asked.

'They'll be fine,' Sammy replied confidently. 'They don't care about sirens. They only care about food and laying eggs. He paused. 'And foxes. They don't like foxes. Have you ever seen a fox, Gio?'

'A few times. Do you think they'll have any at the zoo?'

Sammy screwed up his face. 'Maybe. I want to see a tiger or a lion. They're better than foxes.'

'They're certainly bigger and fiercer,' Gio agreed. 'But do you know what I'm hoping will be there?'

'No, what?'

'Baboons.'

'Why? What are they?'

'A kind of monkey. They've got bright red butts and blue faces.'

Nikki rolled her eyes. Was Gio really talking about monkey's bottoms? But when Sammy sniggered, she realised that Gio had hit exactly the right note with her son, because there was nothing more amusing to an eleven-year-old boy than bottoms. And in that instant she lost another little piece of her heart to the man who already possessed far too much of it.

Nikki smiled indulgently at her son as he waved his fork in the air, and chatted animatedly as he ate.

They had been in the restaurant for half an hour, and Sammy had yet to stop talking.

She didn't mind though, and Gio didn't seem bothered, either. She kept catching his eye and the amused smile in their depths made her heart sing. Going to the zoo had been a brilliant idea, and Gio had been fabulous with Sammy.

Her son had had simply the best time ever, and was now reliving every animal he had seen in technicolour detail.

True to his word, Gio hadn't attempted even one sneaky kiss. He'd not even held her hand. Instead, his attention had been on Sammy, and ensuring that her son enjoyed himself.

On seeing Sammy's face and listening to his excited chatter, Nikki could safely say that he had.

'Can you please stop talking long enough to eat your food?' Nikki begged.

Sammy's plate was still half full, whilst Nikki had almost cleared hers. Stopping off on the way home to have a meal had been another of Gio's suggestions.

'But I'm telling Gio about Princess and Toffee,' Sammy protested. 'It's important.'

Gio nodded. 'It is,' he agreed. 'Looking after two goats is a big responsibility.'

Sammy speared a chip and shoved it into his mouth, hastily eating before saying, 'I take them into the orchard every morning to a different part, and Mum helps me tie them up so they don't wander off, and they eat all the brambles and other stuff, and then I bring them in after tea.'

'Bring them in the house?' Gio asked, wide-eyed.

Sammy gave him a withering hook. 'The **barn**.'

'Oh, I see. **The barn**.' Gio nodded sagely.

'I've got my very own chicken.'

'You have?'

'Yes, Aunty Dulcie gave it to me. She's called Kevin.'

Gio's lips twitched. 'That's an unusual name for a chicken.'

'Kevin de Bayne. He's a footballer,' Sammy informed him.

'I see. I take it you like football?'

'Sammy,' Nikki interrupted. 'Eat your meal. You can talk about football later. Or not at all,' she muttered under her breath.

'Not a footie fan?' Gio asked her, as Sammy obediently popped another forkful of food into his mouth and chewed vigorously.

'Not so much.'

'I've made a friend called Mason,' Sammy announced, his butterfly mind darting to another subject. 'He goes to the stables. Petra says I'm almost as good at riding as he is and he's been doing it for ages. It was only my first go.'

Nikki smiled at the pride in her son's voice. 'Petra is letting him have a lesson or two in exchange for helping out,' she reminded Gio. She wasn't entirely sure how much help Sammy was giving Petra, but she was grateful to the woman for her generosity, nevertheless.

'Next time he has a lesson, I'm going to show him my chicken and the goats. Can I have another lemonade, please?'

Gio caught the waiter's attention and ordered fresh drinks.

'Can Gio come to my birthday party?' Sammy asked. 'I'm going to be twelve.'

Nikki panicked. What party? She hadn't planned on Sammy having a party! She had assumed that a takeaway pizza, a birthday cake, and an evening spent playing the new video game she had bought him, would suffice. He didn't know anyone his own age here, apart from Mason, and he'd only met the boy once.

'Um...we'll see. You do know that it'll only be you, me, Dulcie and Otto, don't you?'

'Walter can come, and Petra,' Sammy added. 'And Gio.'

Nikki sighed. 'I'm sorry, kiddo, there won't be a party as such. Unless...do you want to go home to Birmingham and you can have a proper party? Maybe go to the cinema with a couple of friends? Or how about a paint-balling session, and a pizza afterwards?'

Sammy froze, then he seemed to close in on himself and his eyes grew fearful. 'I don't want to go home. I want to stay here.'

'Then we'll stay,' Nikki said, relief washing over her. She wasn't ready to go home yet, either. 'As long as you don't mind spending your birthday with us grown-ups,' she said.

However, her relief that they were staying a while was tempered by her worry that Sammy was starting to put down roots in Picklewick.

Actually, not Picklewick as such, but Muddypuddle Lane. Between the farm and the stables, Sammy was making himself very much at home, and it was going to be a wrench when they finally did have to leave.

Perhaps staying here for the whole of the summer wasn't the wisest thing she had ever done, but Sammy seemed so happy and was having such a brilliant time that there was no way she could bring herself to cut their holiday short. If he had agreed to go home early to spend his birthday with his friends, that would have been different. But she had seen the way he'd shut down when she suggested it, and had seen the misery that had flashed across his face, and she couldn't do that to him. It would be difficult enough for him when it was time for them to leave at the end of the summer.

It would be difficult for her too, and not solely because of Sammy. She now had her growing feelings for Gio to contend with.

Nikki kissed her son's forehead then tucked the bed covers around his shoulders as Sammy screwed up his face and emitted a huge yawn.

'We had fun today, didn't we?' she said, getting up off the bed.

'I like Gio,' he replied.

So do I, Nikki thought. She smiled vaguely. 'That's good.'

'Do you like him?' her son asked.

'He's nice.'

'Is he your boyfriend?'

Nikki inhaled sharply. 'Whatever gave you that idea?'

'You go gooey when he talks to you.'

'I do not!'

'Mum, you **do**. It's okay, I don't mind.' He yawned again.

'Night, Sammykins.'

'Night, Mum. Tell Aunty Dulcie thank you for bringing Princess and Toffee in.'

'I will.' She switched off the bedside light but left the bedroom door slightly ajar.

He didn't need a light at night, but since he'd started secondary school, he had insisted on one, and it broke her heart to think how fearful he had become over the past academic year.

'Wine?' Dulcie asked, when Nikki walked into the sitting room and plopped down into a chair. The smell of paint lingered in the air, not quite masked by the scented candle her sister had lit.

'I'd love one, please.'

Dulcie poured her a glass of Chardonnay and handed it to her.

'Thanks.' Nikki took it gratefully and sipped at it. 'Mmm, nice.'

'So?' Dulcie leant forward. 'Did you have a good time?'

'It was lovely.'

'How did Sammy get on with Gio?'

'Surprisingly well. Gio's really good with him.' Nikki snorted. 'When I was putting Sammy to bed, he asked if Gio is my boyfriend.'

'It's a legitimate question. Is he?'

'I wouldn't call him a boyfriend as such,' Nikki objected.

'What would you call him? Your lover?'

'No! We haven't— I mean— **No.**'

'Why not?'

Nikki shrugged. 'I don't know him well enough, for one thing.' She smiled wryly. 'And there's the lack of opportunity, for another.'

'Ah-ha! So, if you had the chance you **would** jump into bed with him!'

'Not necessarily.'

'Liar.'

'Okay, I might.'

'Now we're getting somewhere.'

 Nikki put her glass on the coffee table. 'I hate to break it to you, sis, but this...whatever it is—' she waved a hand in the air '—isn't going to go anywhere. He lives here and I live in Birmingham, so...' She didn't need to finish the sentence.

'Remember what I said about letting your hair down and having fun?' Dulcie reminded her. 'This doesn't have to be the love affair to end all love affairs. Just enjoy it for what it is – a holiday romance.'

'I'm not sure I'm cut out for holiday romances. I'm the sort to get too involved.'

'Are you too involved already?'

'I don't know,' she replied honestly. 'Maybe.'

Her phone ringing made her jump, and she scrambled to answer it, worry why someone was calling her at this time of night surging through her. From the look on Dulcie's face, her sister was equally as concerned.

'It's Gio,' she said, with relief, heaving herself out of the chair and going into the hall for some privacy.

'Hi, Gio.'

'Hi, you. Sorry, I know it's late, but we didn't have chance to say a proper goodnight.'

'Goodnight,' she replied softly. 'Is that better?'

'No.'

'I didn't think it would be.'

'Can you sneak away? Just for a few minutes?'

Intrigued, Nikki said, 'I might be able to. Why?'

'I was thinking I could drive up to the farm and meet you at the top of Muddypuddle Lane. Then I can say goodnight to you properly. I can be there in five minutes.'

'Make it ten, and you've got a deal.'

Nikki hurried into the sitting room, picked up her glass and downed the contents.

'What's wrong?' Dulcie asked.

'Nothing. Can you listen out for Sammy? I'm...er...just popping outside for a minute.'

Her sister's eyebrows shot up. 'Booty call?'

'Definitely not. I...um...left something in his car and he's popping it up.'

Dulcie bit her lip. Her eyes were twinkling when she asked, 'What is so important that it can't wait until the next time you see him?'

Nikki thought furiously, but her mind was a blank

Laughing, Dulcie said, 'Take as long as you need.'

Pulse racing, Nikki hot-footed it into the downstairs loo to freshen up, but after raking her fingers through her hair, she studied her reflection in dismay. If anything, she looked worse now than she had two minutes ago. Her cheeks were pink, and her hair was all over the place.

Drat! She didn't have time to renew her make-up or tame her hair – Gio would have to take her as he found her. And she'd no sooner thought it than the sound of an engine could be heard coming up the lane and she hurried outside.

The car came to a halt, and Nikki almost sprinted across the yard in her haste.

Gio got out and came towards her. He didn't say a word. All he did was hold out his arms and she fell into them. Then his mouth found hers and for several long delectable minutes she lost herself in their embrace.

As delightful as it was to be held by him, as they kissed Nikki had become aware of another feeling – that this was where she was meant to be, as though she had found her home – and the knowledge rocked her to her core.

A final kiss, this time a far more gentle peck than the kisses they had just shared, and Nikki was gone, disappearing into the shadows as she headed back to the house. Gio watched her go, the taste of her on his lips, the scent of her in his nose. And although she had only just stepped out of his arms, he longed to hold her again.

It had been a mistake to come back to the farm tonight, he realised, but he hadn't been able to resist. Now he would spend the next few hours thinking about her.

Oh, hell, who was he kidding? He would have thought about her anyway – because since she had returned to Picklewick, he had thought of little else.

Gio had the frightening yet scarily wonderful feeling that he was besotted with her.

He still couldn't fathom how he had got himself into this position. One minute he had been happily living his life and minding his own business, and the next he had smiled at a gorgeous woman whilst he had been waiting at the pedestrian crossing for the lights to change.

And that might have been the end of it, but for a trip to the stables on Muddypuddle Lane on a bank holiday Monday in May.

Even then, he hadn't anticipated seeing her again until he'd bumped into Dulcie Fairfax...

And the rest, they say, was history.

Today had been fun though, and he wasn't just referring to the last twenty minutes. He had enjoyed the visit to the zoo immensely, and he had enjoyed spending time with her son. Sammy was a good kid and a credit to her. He was polite, funny, inquisitive, and friendly, with a hint of pre-teenage sass. Gio had sensed sadness and anxiety too, just below the surface, and he guessed it was because of the bullying. Even if it had been resolved to Nikki's satisfaction, it was bound to leave a scar. But it hadn't as yet, she had informed him, although she was hoping for a resolution before the new term started next month, so the child's anxiety was probably through the roof. Thank goodness Sammy was here for the summer, because it was taking his mind off his problems for a while.

Gio's heart went out to the poor kid and he wished it was in his power to do something to help, but there was nothing he **could** do. Just make any time they were together as enjoyable as possible. For Nikki, too, because he could tell how much it hurt her to know her son was so unhappy.

His thoughts turned to Sammy's forthcoming birthday, and how the child preferred to spend it with a bunch of old fogies rather than return home and have a party with his friends, and he wondered if there was something he could do to make the day special.

He had no idea what kind of things kids Sammy's age were into, but many of his colleagues had children, so perhaps he could pick their brains.

'I've got an idea for Sammy's birthday,' Gio said, several days later. 'If it's okay with you.'

Nikki knew that when she agreed to go to Gio's house for a meal this evening that it wouldn't just be food she would be hungry for, and after he'd invited her in, she had fully expected him to whisk her off to bed, especially after the passionate welcome he had just given her. What she hadn't expected was to talk about Sammy's birthday.

'What is it?' she asked, breathless and trembling, as he led her into the lounge.

'A car driving experience.'

'Er...right.' She tilted her face up to his to be kissed again, which he did, but immediately afterwards he was back on the subject of Sammy's birthday again, much to her disappointment.

'Before you say anything, it's not the sort of driving experience you can buy online. And it won't cost you a penny, either,' he told her.

'How come?' Her interest was piqued, despite wishing he would shut up and make love to her.

She had arranged for a cake to be made by Megan, but that was as far as she'd got. Which was unfortunate, considering Sammy's birthday was fast approaching, and although she had batted some ideas around, such as camping on top of the mountain and cooking sausages on an open fire, or a visit to a theme park followed by a birthday tea, which would naturally consist of pizza (Sammy's favourite), she had yet to make a decision. It was very unlike her to be so disorganised, but being at the farm had thrown her a bit.

'I've had a word with the owner of a private airfield nearby, and he's agreed to let me use the airstrip for a couple of hours,' Gio was saying.

Nikki wasn't sure she understood. 'I don't follow...?'

'I've called in a favour from someone in the DTU – sorry, Driver Training Agency – and he has agreed to sign out one of the training vehicles so Sammy can have a go in it. He won't be allowed to drive it, but he will be able to sit in it whilst Dean takes the car through its paces. It's all perfectly safe – Dean is a police driving instructor and he knows what he's doing. Then, if Sammy wants, and you are happy for him to do so, he can have a go at driving my car around the airfield.'

Nikki blinked. 'Gosh, I don't know what to say. He'll love that. Thank you.'

Gio grinned. 'I was hoping you'd say that.'

'I suppose I'd better thank you properly,' she said, and abruptly the atmosphere changed.

'What were you thinking of?' His voice was hoarse, and the sound of it made her go all tingly.

'This,' she said, kissing him briefly on the lips. 'And this...' She trailed kisses down his neck. 'Maybe this.' She nibbled her way along his collarbone, drawing his shirt to one side. 'How am I doing so far?'

'You're getting there,' he murmured.

She felt a shiver go through him as his arms came around her, and she looked into his eyes. Her stomach clenched at the hunger she saw in them, and her breath caught as she waited for him to act, her excitement building with each beat of her heart.

Finally, finally, his head lowered.

His mouth hard on hers, the kiss deep and desperate, she frantically reached for the buttons on his shirt, her fingers trembling as she scrabbled to undo them, feeling his hands slide underneath her blouse, sensing his urgency as he met her passion with equal ardour.

'Not here,' he growled.

Then he scooped her up and carried her to his bed.

Nikki's breathing was slow and deep, and every so often she would make a cute little whimpering noise in her sleep. And whenever she did, Gio held her closer until she settled again.

He knew he would have to wake her soon, but not yet, not when he was enjoying watching her sleep and luxuriating in the feel of her body against his. She was curled into him, her cheek on his shoulder, one hand resting on his chest, one leg entwined in his. Her hair tickled his nose, but he didn't want to brush it away and risk disturbing her. She looked so peaceful. There was even a small smile on her lips, and he hoped he was responsible for it being there.

She had certainly put a smile on his face. And not just because they'd made love –

although that had been one of the most heady experiences of his life. He loved being with her. He felt alive when he was with her, as though the time spent before he'd met her had been lived in a shadow that he hadn't known he was under until now.

He wanted to make love to her again, but he didn't move a muscle, wanting to freeze this moment, to capture it forever, and never let her go.

This woman had taken his breath away, and if he had suspected that he might be half in love with her before this, he realised he was fully in love with her now.

Craning his neck, he checked the time. It was late, or should he say 'early'? Dawn wasn't far off, and he knew Nikki wanted to be home before Sammy woke.

Home...

He snorted softly. The farm wasn't her home, Picklewick wasn't her village. All too soon she would be going home for real, and he didn't know how he was going to deal with that.

Was this how it was always going to be, this relationship of theirs? Her always having to leave, him always having to say goodbye?

You're a fool, Gio, he said to himself. But it was too late now, the damage was done. He had already lost his heart to her, and he was terrified she might break it.

There was no **might** about it – she **would** break it, through no fault of her own.

If it was anyone's fault, it was his, for falling in love with her in the first place, despite vowing that he wouldn't get too involved. And what had happened to his new philosophy of living for the moment and not dwelling on the future?

Heartache would be the cost, so all he could do was follow his own advice and concentrate on the present and how happy she made him.

And with that, Gio woke her gently, with the softest of kisses, and when they had made love again, it was with a heavy heart that he watched her leave, knowing that all too soon he would be forced to watch her leave for good.

CHAPTER EIGHT

'This is the best birthday ever!' Sammy declared, as he shovelled the rest of his pizza into his mouth. 'Kaneyavagog.'

'Don't speak with your mouth full,' Nikki told him. 'Would you like to repeat that?' she suggested, after he hastily swallowed what he was eating.

'I said, can I have a dog?' He smiled hopefully.

'Don't push your luck, buster,' she warned. 'You've got a chicken.'

'Yes, but Kevin lives **here**, not with us.'

'You're at school all day and I'm at work, so if we did have a dog, who would take care of it?'

Sammy scowled. 'I don't **have** to go to school. I could stay home and look after it.'

Nikki clamped down on the sigh that threatened to escape. Why did he have to bring this up now? They'd had such a lovely day, and now Sammy was threatening to end his birthday on a sour note.

She had been aware for a couple of days that as the date for returning home loomed ever larger, Sammy was beginning to withdraw into his shell again. He had been his old self today, full of bubbling energy and wide-eyed delight, the opportunity to drive Gio's car being the highlight, even surpassing the high-speed rally-type driving that Dean had done, which had Sammy shrieking and screaming with pretend terror and a great deal of glee.

They had stopped off at a traditional ice cream parlour afterwards, for a sandwich and a knickerbocker glory, accompanied by a large glass of fizzy red pop, then it was back to the farm for a kickabout with the football Gio had bought him, followed by a session playing his new game, which had ended up being a hard-fought competition between him and Gio. Sammy had won and had been jubilant (and Nikki had quietly thanked Gio for letting him win). After that, they had ordered pizza with sides.

They – and by 'they' she meant Sammy, Gio, Dulcie, Otto, Otto's dad Walter, and herself – were just finishing the meal, with the intention of bringing the birthday cake out, when Sammy's mood had abruptly soured.

Nikki winced apologetically as her son sat back in his seat and folded his arms.

'We've discussed this, Sammy,' she said. 'I have to go to work, and you have to go to school.' And when he opened his mouth to argue, she shook her head in warning and he subsided sullenly.

'Cake time?' Dulcie mouthed.

'Good idea.' Nikki started clearing away the pizza boxes and the rest of the debris, to make room on the table.

'Let me help,' Gio offered, getting to his feet, and picking up the haphazardly stacked cartons.

Nikki trotted into the kitchen, anxious to light the sparkler on top of the cake, which would hopefully take her son's mind off his problems for a while longer. Gio followed her out, and as soon as he had divested himself of the rubbish he was carrying, he gathered her to him.

It felt good being in his arms, hearing the steady throb of his heart, feeling the solidity of his chest against her cheek. If only she could stay there forever, but she had to go home in a matter of days, and, like her son, she was dreading it. Not only was she having to leave a man she was fairly sure she had fallen in love with, but Sammy's misery would be almost impossible to bear.

She had tried phoning the school again yesterday, without any luck, because the call had gone unanswered even though she knew that staff would have been on site because that was the day the exam results were out. So she had been forced to send an email instead. She was still waiting for a response, but she guessed that she wouldn't get one until the middle of next week, because Monday was a bank holiday.

Unable to contain her worry, she let out a sob. 'He's so unhappy,' she cried.

'It'll be okay,' Gio murmured into her hair.

'You can't know that,' she snapped. Then said, 'Sorry. I shouldn't take my frustration out on you.'

'I don't mind. And you're right – platitudes don't help.'

Nikki lifted her head. 'What if the bullying carries on? He's adamant that he doesn't want to go to another school, but for his own sake I can't let him remain in this one. I'm beginning to wonder if I **should** give up work and home school him. After all, money isn't everything.' She screwed up her face. 'We would end up losing the house, though.'

'Maybe the school is in the middle of arranging for this other kid to go somewhere else, but it hasn't been finalised yet and they don't want to contact you until they've got some definite news?'

Nikki appreciated that Gio was trying to rationalise the delay, but she didn't believe it for one second. 'I'll just have to hope that's the case, won't I?'

'Come on, wipe your eyes. It won't do Sammy any good to see you upset.'

Nikki knew Gio was right. Grabbing a piece of kitchen towel, she dabbed her eyes, then blew her nose. Getting upset wasn't going to help, and there was a birthday cake to cut.

She opened the lid of the box and was just about to take the cake out, when she felt Gio's arms slide around her waist, and she squirmed around to face him, her lips meeting his for the briefest of kisses.

'Mum, what are—? **Oh...**'

Nikki and Gio leapt apart, Nikki's cheeks flaming. How stupid of her! To be caught kissing Gio, and by Sammy no less! What must he think of her?

'Er...Sammy, Gio was just...um...' she began, before she ran out of words.

Sammy gave her the kind of look that told her he knew exactly what she and Gio had been doing.

'Go back into the dining room, I'll be out in a second,' she said.

'Come on, mate.' Gio ushered Sammy out of the kitchen. 'It's time to sing happy birthday.'

Sammy glanced over his shoulder at her, but his expression was unreadable, and her heart sank.

Plastering a smile on her face, she lit the sparkler, picked up the cake, and walked slowly into the dining room, bursting into a rather wobbly rendition of **Happy Birthday to You** as she did so.

Everyone joined in and clapped when the cake was cut, but Nikki's attention was firmly on her son, wondering what was going through his mind.

She felt mortified, and guilty, too. The poor boy didn't need to have seen that. Two minutes previously he had been telling her just how much he didn't want to go to school, and then he catches her making out with a man who was only supposed to be a friend.

Sammy must think that she wasn't taking his concerns and feelings seriously.

As soon as she got him on his own, she would make sure that he knew he was the most important person in her life and that his happiness was the only thing that mattered.

To her astonishment though, she needn't have worried.

After saying a subdued and low-key goodnight to Gio, Nikki went in search of her son, who was saying his own goodnight to a couple of goats.

She found him in the barn, sitting on a pile of straw, staring at Princess. Puss was also there, but as usual the cat kept its distance.

'Sammy...' she began.

He looked around. 'Hi, Mum.'

She sat down next to him. 'About Gio...' She was about to tell him 'It isn't what you think' but she didn't want to insult his intelligence. So instead, she said, 'I'm sorry you had to see that.'

'You were kissing him.'

'I was.'

'You said he isn't your boyfriend.'

She took a deep breath. 'To be honest, I'm not sure what he is.'

'Will you be sad when we go home?'

'A bit,' she admitted. 'It's been fun here, hasn't it?'

'I don't want to leave.'

'I know you don't, Sammykins.'

For once, he didn't object to the endearment, and she put an arm around his shoulders and hugged him to her.

'I promise you, that one way or another we'll get it sorted, but before we do anything drastic, let's see what the school has to say first, eh?'

He scooted around to face her. 'Will Gio come to visit us?'

'I doubt it. We live too far away, but I expect we'll bump into him the next time we come to the farm.'

'When?'

'I don't know. We can't descend on Aunty Dulcie every holiday.'

His mouth turned down and his expression grew even more troubled. 'I like Gio. He's cool.'

'So do I, Sammy, so do I.'

'What if we never see him again? Will you be sad?'

'Yes, I will,' she replied honestly. She would be sadder than she ever thought possible.

Determined to make the most of their final day together, Gio suggested going for a picnic on the mountain: all three of them, because he'd miss the little guy almost as much as he would miss the boy's mother.

The day was a glorious one, the air warm and clear, and to give themselves a breather (because it was a bit of a hike to the top) they had stopped to pick some of the blueberries that grew wild on the slopes above the farm.

'Can you really eat these?' Sammy asked, as he held up a fat berry. He was sitting amongst the heather and the blueberry bushes, looking incredulous. His fingers were already stained purple, and they had only started picking a few minutes ago.

'You really can,' Gio said, popping one in his mouth. 'Mmm, sweet and juicy. Try one.'

Sammy looked to his mother for confirmation that it was okay, and Nikki nodded.

She was looking even more gorgeous than usual, in a red sleeveless dress and a matching red sunhat. Her shoulders were bare, the skin lightly tanned, and so were her legs. She looked fresh and summery, and Gio couldn't believe that the summer holidays were nearly at an end. She and Sammy were going home tomorrow, and he wasn't ready to let her go.

He didn't think he ever would be.

But leave she would, and he had to accept it.

To add insult to injury, the weather today was absolutely glorious, the summer not done with them yet, despite the first of September being only three days away. The new academic year would start on Monday, Sammy would be back in school, and for Gio life would go back to the way it had been before he had met Nikki.

Except...it wouldn't be the same at all. She had changed him irrevocably, and it was both a sadness and a joy.

At the moment, sadness was winning, as he glanced at her to find her gazing back at him. His heart clenched, the pain of her loss already piercing his heart and she hadn't even left yet.

Sammy soon ran out of the patience that was needed to pick enough blueberries to make it worthwhile, but the three of them combined their efforts into one tub, and probably had enough to make a few muffins. Or rather, Otto would make the muffins, but that wouldn't be until after Nikki and Sammy had left.

There it was again: **left**. It kept popping into his mind, however hard he tried to pretend it wasn't happening.

Gio straightened up, his back aching from bending over to reach the berries. 'Shall we wash our hands in the stream, then we can have our picnic?' He waggled fingers that were covered in sticky blueberry juice.

The stream trickled down the hillside in the little valley it had carved out for itself over the course of hundreds of years, and the tinkling call of the water proved irresistible to Sammy. The boy was soon racing leaves, twigs and anything else he could get his hands on down it, before he turned his attention to building a small dam.

'This is perfect, thank you,' Nikki said as she sank down into the springy grass.

Gio sat next to her, watching the child's antics. 'I'm going to miss you,' he said.

'Don't, please don't. Can we just enjoy today and not think about tomorrow?' Her eyes glittered with unshed tears, and he felt like crying too.

'I'll try. It's not easy.'

'No, it's not.' She plucked a blade of grass and began shredding it, peeling it apart down the length of its stem, her gaze on Sammy.

'Let's eat,' Gio suggested. Although he didn't feel in the least bit hungry, he guessed that Sammy probably was.

And whilst the adults nibbled and picked at their food, Sammy wolfed down the selection of sandwiches and savoury pastries that Gio had bought from the delicatessen in the village, followed by a couple of slices of birthday cake that was left over from the other day.

After they'd eaten, the three of them carried on up the hillside until they reached the top, where they took in the view.

'Look, Sammy.' Nikki pointed to some specks far below. 'Is that Petra taking people out on a hack?'

'I'm a really good rider now, aren't I, Mum?' Sammy announced proudly.

'You are!' she enthused.

'I'm surprised Sammy didn't persuade you to have a go,' Gio laughed.

Nikki pulled a face. 'I can just about cope with the goats. Horses are a bit too big for my liking. Maybe next time.'

 She turned stricken eyes to him, and pain lanced his chest when he realised that it had been a slip of the tongue, and that there probably wouldn't be a next time. Not like this.

When she did return to Muddypuddle Lane, they wouldn't simply pick up where they left off.

This was it, the end. Once today was over, their relationship would be, too. And his heart would be well and truly broken.

Never had anything felt more bitter-sweet, Nikki thought.

Her head lay on Gio's chest, and their limbs were entangled, the sheets bunched and crumpled from their lovemaking.

Wild, frantic and desperate love had been peppered with tender softness, until she had sobbed with the joy and the sadness of it.

If she had known that saying goodbye would hurt this much, she would never have given in to her desire. But then, she would never have got to know this remarkable man. She would have denied herself the ecstasy that loving him had brought her. And there was no getting away from the reality that she loved him.

Love had crept up on her, sneakily insidious, until she had been well and truly caught.

So much for this only being a no-strings summer fling.

Technically, that was all it was, but emotionally it was much, much more. And like Sandy from **Grease**, Nikki was totally devoted to Gio. But that was where any similarity ended. Unlike Sandy, Nikki couldn't change her whole life for Gio. This wasn't a high school teenage crush; this was real life with real responsibilities. She had a mortgage and a job, and her life wasn't in Picklewick, however much she wished it was.

She had gone into this well aware of the limitations of their romance, and now that autumn was on its way, she had to accept that in a few short minutes their relationship would be well and truly over.

Gio stirred, and she lifted her head to find him looking at her, the love and pain she felt mirrored in his eyes.

Blinking back tears – there would be plenty of time to let them fall when she was at home – she reluctantly sat up. It was time.

'Stay. **Please**.' Gio put a hand on her thigh.

'You know I can't. It'll be light soon. I've got to get back.'

'I meant, stay in Picklewick. Don't go back to Birmingham,' he pleaded.

'You know I can't,' she repeated. 'There's my house, my job, my—'

'I love you.'

Nikki hitched in a ragged breath, the tears that she had been trying so hard to hold back, spilling over and trickling down her cheeks.

Why did he have to say that? **Why?**

'I mean it. I love you,' he repeated, and she knew it was true.

'I love you too,' she croaked. Clearing her throat, her voice thick with emotion, she added, 'But it doesn't change anything. It can't.'

'I know.' He sounded as broken as she.

Unable to bear it and worried that she might totally break down, Nikki slipped out of bed and reached for her clothes.

Gio made to get up.

'Stay there,' she instructed. 'I want to remember you just like this.'

He subsided, naked, back onto the bed, and her gaze raked him as she tried to commit every detail to memory.

He watched as she pulled on her jeans and tee shirt, misery and resignation on his face. 'Is this it? Is this how it ends?' He shook his head, as though refusing to believe it.

'It has to. We can't— It's not—' She stopped abruptly.

They both knew the score. She had made no secret of the fact that she was only here for the summer. Neither had promised the other anything more.

Yet, here they were, hearts breaking.

They were old enough to know better, but they had acted like a pair of teenagers and now they had to pay the price.

'I love you,' he said, for the third time, his voice breaking.

'I love you, too.'

For long seconds they stared at each other. Tears trickled down Nikki's face, and she let them fall as Gio swiped a hand across his cheeks, his eyes wet and glistening.

Then, without another word, she turned on her heel and walked out of the room, her heart breaking with the knowledge that she would probably never see him again.

'It's a bit big, but you'll grow into it,' Nikki said in the time-honoured fashion of mothers everywhere when faced with having to buy a new school blazer for their child.

Sammy modelled the blazer sullenly, his arms dangling by his sides, his shoulders drooping. Nikki tried not to react to the despair on his face, but she couldn't help feeling equally as miserable.

'How does it feel?' she asked, going behind him to check the fit at the back.

He shrugged.

'Do you think it's too big?'

He didn't respond, so she turned to the shop assistant. Nikki had left it rather late – with the autumn term starting on Monday, most parents had already kitted their kids out with new school uniform, and there wasn't a great deal left. It was either this size, or Sammy would have to make do with his old one, which was now way too small for him, she had discovered when she'd told him to try it on. Sammy had shot up over the summer. Nikki blamed it on all that fresh air

The summer...

Best not think about it. Not right now. Not if she didn't want to burst into tears in the middle of Castor's Outfitters.

'As you said,' the shop assistant replied, 'he'll grow into it. Better too big, than not big enough.'

She sounded bored, and Nikki guessed the poor woman must have repeated the same thing hundreds of times over the course of the last few weeks.

'We'll take it,' Nikki decided. She didn't want to shell out for a new blazer, but she didn't have a lot of choice. It was the only one left in this size, and if she didn't buy it on the off-chance that she might be forced to look for another school for Sammy and therefore it wouldn't be needed and he ended up staying in his current school instead, then the odds were that the blazer would be snapped up by another parent and Sammy would end up wearing his woefully too-small old one.

'Shoes,' she said, clapping her hands together with forced jollity.

Sammy glared at her balefully.

'And a new PE kit,' she added. He could probably get away with the one he had for a few more months, but she was hoping a new footie shirt might cheer him up.

No such luck.

Her son endured the uniform buying trip in silence, only speaking to her when Nikki forced him to. Even then, most of his responses were in the form of a shrug or a flattening of his lips.

'McDonald's?' she suggested as they went outside. Laden down with bags, she'd had her fill of shopping, but as Sammy still had to find a pair of shoes (Castors hadn't had his size) Nikki needed a sit down and some sustenance, before diving back into the fray once more.

Even the offer of a Big Mac and fries was met with stony silence, but she took him for one anyway.

'How would you like it if Aunty Maisie looked after you for a couple of hours tomorrow?' she asked brightly.

Sammy stared at his food. He had done little more than pick at it.

'I'm going to see Mrs Harcastle,' Nikki explained, 'and I asked Aunty Maisie if she would pop around for a couple of hours while I'm out. Or would you prefer to go to Nanny's instead?'

'Don't care,' he grunted.

It would be less hassle to have Maisie babysit Sammy in his own house, rather than trek halfway across the city to her mum's, Nikki decided.

She was disappointed not to have heard a peep from the school, and with the pupils due to start back on Monday, Nikki wanted an answer. Tomorrow was a teacher training day, when all the staff would be preparing for the new term, and Nikki was confident that the headteacher would also be there.

Having been unable to contact the school, Nikki felt she had no choice other than to turn up and refuse to leave until she had spoken to the woman. She was aware that her actions might be regarded as confrontational, but she felt she didn't have any choice.

One way or another, she was going to sort this out. Nikki mightn't be able to do anything to ease the pain in her own heart, but she would do her utmost to lighten the pain in her son's.

'As a teacher yourself, I'm sure you understand that these things take time, and what with the summer holidays—'

'With the greatest respect,' Nikki interrupted the headteacher, 'I am well aware that the Department of Education continues to function throughout August, and that headteachers rarely take the full six weeks off. What I don't understand is how it can take so long to make a decision regarding this boy.'

'As I said—'

Nikki got to her feet. 'This isn't getting us anywhere. You have been unable to deal with the situation at a school level, therefore any future assault by Blake will necessitate me calling the police, and I will also be making a formal complaint about the school's failure in its duty of care regarding my son. Do I make myself clear?' She knew she sounded officious but being polite and reasonable hadn't worked.

'Perfectly.' The woman's reply was frosty.

'Good!' And with that Nikki marched out of the headteacher's office.

She was so upset she could cry, despite already guessing even before she had spoken to Mrs Hardcastle today that nothing had been done. And probably never would be. It would take another incident and for her threat of going to the police to become a reality, before the school would set the ball rolling to remove Sammy's bully from the school, because Nikki didn't believe for one second that the bullying would stop unless drastic action was taken.

And because she wasn't prepared to put her son in harm's way again, she had a decision to make. A big one. One which would have serious consequences for her financially, but one which would benefit Sammy's mental health enormously. And that decision was whether to take him out of school altogether and educate him herself, or move him to another school and hope he would settle there.

But, in her heart, she already knew what she was going to do.

As she drove home, Nikki decided not to say anything to Sammy just yet. She needed to think this through properly, because if she did pack in her job as a supply teacher in order to home educate him, she would be without an income and she wouldn't be able to pay the mortgage. Therefore it was imperative that she found work of some description. Maybe she could find a job working from home, or do private tutoring? Or evening work in a bar or a restaurant, if her mum would babysit Sammy. It was a lot to think about, and she only had the weekend in which to do it.

'How did it go?' Maisie asked, when Nikki arrived home.

Her youngest sister was curled up in a chair, reading a magazine.

Nikki pulled a face. 'Not good. Where's Sammy?'

'In his room. He's been as good as gold. You'd be proud of me: I didn't let him play on his Xbox the whole time you were out – we had a geography lesson.'

Nikki slung her bag on the sofa and dropped down next to it. 'What did he teach you?' she asked wryly.

'Ha ha. Very funny. **Not**. I did the teaching, actually. He wanted to know where Picklewick was on the map.' Maisie wrapped a lock of hair around her finger and twirled it. 'I was thinking of going to visit Dulcie again.'

Nikki closed her eyes and rested her head against the cushion. The thought of what she was about to do made her feel ill. How she wished she could turn the clock back to this time last week. Her problems had seemed smaller, less real, and although she knew it had been an illusion, she would give anything to be there and not here.

She would also give anything to be in Gio's arms, but that was a place she could never return to except in her dreams, so she pushed the thought firmly away as she felt the familiar prickle in the back of her eyes.

'I can catch the train to Thornbury, and a bus from there to Picklewick,' Maisie was saying. 'We looked it up. We also did a few distance calculations, so I squeezed in some maths, too! Maybe I should look at teaching...'

Maisie had considered several careers since she'd left college, but teaching hadn't been one of them.

'Maybe you should,' Nikkie replied, keeping her tone neutral. Maisie was a dreamer, a free-spirit, flitting from one thing to the next, and Nikki had little hope of her settling on anything any time soon.

She blamed their mother – Maisie was the youngest of the four siblings and Mum had babied her something rotten. It wouldn't have been a problem if the babying had tailed off as Maisie grew up, but it hadn't, and Nikki's sister still acted as though she was a teenager, despite being twenty-five. It didn't help that she still lived at home and partied like she was eighteen. Saying that though, Nikki couldn't remember partying as hard as Maisie did when she had been eighteen.

'Will Dulcie mind if I visit her, do you think?' Maisie asked.

'Mum wouldn't be going with you?'

'I'm not sure she can get the time off – which was why I was looking at train times.'

Nikki's spidey-senses perked up. The last time Maisie had gone to the farm, their mum had gone with her and they had driven down in Mum's car. It wasn't like Maisie to be so proactive, and Nikki guessed something was afoot. 'Talking about taking time off, how is the job going?'

'Don't ask.'

'Don't tell me you've lost another job!' Nikki cried.

'Okay, I won't.'

'You **have**, haven't you? Does Mum know?'

'No, and you can't tell her. I'll find another one soon enough.'

Nikki puffed out her cheeks in exasperation. Her sister changed jobs more frequently than most people changed their socks. Maisie seemed to have no difficulty **getting** them – her issue was holding **onto** them.

Maisie's problem was that she was easily bored, and had yet to find anything to hold her interest. She was the same with men. Although Maisie wasn't promiscuous in that she didn't sleep around, she seemed to have a different boyfriend every other week, as she grew bored of those easily, too.

'Do you want to stay for a while? Join us for tea?' Nikki offered, recognising the futility of remonstrating with her.

'No, thanks. I'm going out later, so I need to go home and have a shower.' Maisie gathered her things and as Nikki showed her out, she yelled 'Bye, Sammy!' up the stairs.

When Maisie didn't receive a reply, she shrugged. 'I bet he's got his headphones on. Tell him I said goodbye.'

'I will, and thanks for minding him.'

'It was fun. He's a good kid.'

I know, Nikki thought, closing the door behind her. And he deserved to be able to go to school without being scared out of his wits.

She checked the time before opening her laptop: she would begin tea in an hour or so, but before that she had research to do and plans to make.

Flipping heck, was that the time?

Nikki closed the lid of the laptop and gathered up the notes she had made, shuffling them into a neat pile. It was nearly five-thirty and she had been so engrossed in her research that over two hours had gone by. Sammy would be clamouring for his tea soon.

Stiffly, she got to her feet and rubbed her sore eyes. Her brain was whirling and she briefly thought about resuming where she'd left off after they'd eaten, but she was too tired to concentrate any more today. She had made some headway though, which she was pleased about. On the new school front, there was one that she definitely liked the look of. It would be a struggle to get him into it because it was oversubscribed, but she would give it a go if she could convince Sammy it was a good idea.

As for home schooling, her best option financially (but the one she liked the least) was for her and Sammy to move back in with her mum and rent her house out. The rent would provide some much-needed income, and her mum would be a built-in babysitter if Nikki was forced to go out to work in the evening. Of course, she had to run that by her mum first, who mightn't be too keen on the idea, which was why she didn't intend to say anything to Sammy yet. She didn't want to get his hopes up needlessly.

Nikki wandered into the kitchen, wondering what they could have for tea instead of the tagine she had planned on cooking. It would have to be something quick and easy – the poor kid must be starving. Then after Sammy had gone to bed she intended to open a cheap bottle of plonk and stare mindlessly at the TV for a couple of hours and try not to think about Gio.

The nights were the worst, she discovered. And so far she had spent three long, interminably lonely nights thinking about him since she'd returned home, with the prospect of many more to come.

Stop thinking about him, she admonished silently. She needed to focus on her son's happiness, not her own.

Before she started cooking, she decided to pop her head around Sammy's bedroom door. Feeling guilty for letting him play video games for the biggest part of the afternoon, and realising she had been so engrossed in finding a solution to his schooling problem that she hadn't seen him since she'd returned from her meeting with the headteacher, she climbed the stairs.

'Sammy?'

He didn't answer her knock, but she didn't expect him to: if he had his headphones on, he would be oblivious even if a brass band was playing outside his window, so she pushed the door open.

He wasn't in his room and his screen was dark.

'Sammy?' she called.

He must be in the bathroom, but when she looked across the landing, the door was open and that room was empty, too.

So was her bedroom, the kitchen, the garden, and the shed.

Sammy was nowhere to be seen.

Her mouth dry and with a coil of fear beginning to unfurl in her belly, Nikki checked every room again, even looking under the beds and in the cupboard under the stairs.

And when she noticed that his backpack and coat had gone, along with his favourite trainers, she had an awful feeling she knew what had happened.

A final check of his money box confirmed her suspicion.

Sammy had run away.

CHAPTER NINE

This was too much, too soon, Gio thought as he stepped out of the shower and towelled himself dry. What had he been thinking when he'd agreed to go on a double date this evening, and a blind one at that.

He was tempted to message Harvey and cancel, but it was a bit short notice and it wouldn't be fair on either Harvey and his girlfriend, or the woman he was supposed to be meeting. He would just have to bite the bullet, don his game face and be on his best behaviour for the duration.

Harvey, the daft bloke, was doing his best to cheer Gio up, but Gio wasn't ready to be cheered. All he wanted was to wallow in misery for the foreseeable future, but Harvey could be a right naggy git when he wanted to be, and he'd kept on, and on, and on, until Gio had agreed. Honestly, after two solid days of Harvey bipping in his ear, Gio would have agreed to anything if it shut the fella up.

The choice of venue wasn't the best, either. The Black Horse was his local, which might have been why Harvey had suggested it, but the pub held far too many memories of Nikki.

Hell, **everywhere** held too many memories, and not least was his very own bed. He kept seeing her there, her hair fanned across the pillow, her eyes with that smoky, sultry hunger that drove him nuts, inviting him to make love to her again.

Jeez, it hurt! To think he would never hold her again, never kiss her, never again tell her he loved her.

So many times during the past few days, he had reached for his phone, desperate to hear her voice, only to put it down again.

It was over. No matter how hard it was to believe, he had to accept it. They were done. He had to get on with his life as best he could without her in it. He was sure that in time the ache would lessen, but for now, it was a heart-stabbing reminder of what could have been, if only their situations were different.

He had even toyed with the idea of putting his house on the market and asking for a transfer to West Midlands Police, but he was held back by the fear that for Nikki this had only been a summer romance after all, and such a grand gesture might horrify her. What if he'd read their relationship wrong? What if he had read **her** wrong?

Despondent and heartsore, he finished towelling himself off and squirted a spray of aftershave across his chest, and wondered once again why he was going out this evening.

The sound of his phone ringing lifted his spirits a little, but only because he hoped it was Harvey calling to cancel. Or it might be work? He could always live in hope...

It was neither, and when he saw who was phoning him, his heart missed a beat before catching up with itself and making him cough. His throat constricted as he answered the call, and he coughed again.

'Gio? **Gio?** Are you there?'

The familiar voice made him want to cry...but wait, was **she** crying?

'Nikki? What's wrong? What's happened?'

Her wail of anguish sent a cold shiver down his spine.

'It's Sammy,' she hiccupped. 'He has run away and it's all my fault! I should have told him I wasn't going to send him back to school and I should have realised how upset he was but I didn't, and he—'

'Shhh, my love, slow down. Start at the beginning.'

He heard her gulp back a sob before she repeated, 'Sammy has run away.'

'When?'

'Today.'

'I know this sounds patronising, but are you sure?'

'Yes.' She drew in a shuddering breath. 'He has taken all the money out of his piggy bank.'

'What time did you notice he was missing?'

'About half an hour ago.'

'How long ago do you think he left?'

'I'm not sure!' she sobbed. 'It could be as long as three or four hours. It's my fault, I should have—'

'Let's not talk about whose fault it is, let's concentrate on getting him home.

Again, at the risk of being patronising, have you phoned his friends? Your mum?' He hesitated. 'How about his father?'

'My mum was the first person I called. He's not there, and he's not with his father. His father doesn't want to know, so he would never have gone to him. None of his friends have seen him. Oh god...I should call the police.'

'That's a good idea,' Gio agreed gently. She should have done that before she phoned him. 'What's your address? I'll be there as soon as I can.'

'No! You don't understand! I **know** where he's going. He is heading to **Picklewick**. Please find him for me, please, **please**...Find my son, before anything happens to him.'

'I will,' he promised. 'I'll find him and bring him back to you.'

But as Gio hurried to get dressed, he hoped with all his heart that he could keep his promise.

'Maisie?' Nikki opened the door to see her sister standing on her step. 'Have you—?' She looked past her, hoping to see Sammy, but Maisie was alone.

'It's all my fault,' Maisie said, her voice breaking. 'I should never have told him how to get to Picklewick on the train.'

Nikki wanted to yell at her that she most definitely shouldn't have, but how could Maisie have known what Sammy would do, when the very idea of him running away hadn't crossed his own mother's mind?

'Can you stay here?' Nikki demanded. After she'd spoken to Gio, she had tried to get hold of Dulcie, but there was no answer, so she'd left a message. She had also called the stables on Muddypuddle Lane and had managed to speak to Petra, who had promised to pop up to the farm and track Dulcie down. She had been just about to phone the police when Maisie had turned up.

'You don't need to ask,' Maisie said. 'I'll stay here as long as you need me.'

'Good. Call the police, report him missing and tell them what's happened. Tell them he's making his way to Picklewick by train. They might be able to track which train he caught.' Nikki grabbed her bag and shoved her feet into her trainers.

'Why? What are you going to do? **Nikki!** Where are you going?'

'To Picklewick, to find Sammy. Don't try to stop me,' she warned.

And god help anyone else who tried – which was why she wanted Maisie to phone the police for her. Nikki had seen enough tv programmes in her time to know that they would want to keep her here, answering endless questions, when all she wanted to do was to get out there and find Sammy.

'Call me if there is any news,' she cried, dashing to the door, snatching her car keys off the table as she flew past.

'Of course, but don't you think—?'

'No, I bloody don't!' she shrieked as she ran outside. There were still a few hours of daylight left, and if she could interrogate Siri on the way, she might have an idea of how frequently the trains ran.

If she was quick — and lucky — depending on what time train he caught and if there were no road works and the traffic was light, she might, **just might**, arrive in Picklewick ahead of her son.

Gio was well aware of police procedures in the case of runaway children, and he knew that even with a possible destination, they would most likely start with Sammy's home as a base and try to track his movements from there. Gio also had no doubt that his local force would also be contacted, but all this would take time.

He might be off duty but he was in Picklewick already, and the first thing he intended to do was to drive up to the farm. Nikki had told him that Sammy would most likely have caught a bus from their house to Birmingham New Street station, and depending on which train he'd caught, he might have to change once or twice, before he ended up in Thornbury. Then it would be another bus ride to Picklewick, followed by a walk from the village to the farm. Gio highly doubted that the boy would take a taxi, but as he raced towards the farm, he radioed in to ask if someone could check with the local taxi office that no one had picked up a twelve-year-old boy who was travelling alone this evening.

Gio was also fairly certain that even if Sammy had made it as far as Muddypuddle Lane, the child wouldn't make his presence known. Sammy would probably slip into the barn or one of the sheds and hope no one would find him. Gio also guessed that Sammy wouldn't have thought much beyond getting to the farm itself, and it would only be when he was cold and hungry that he would realise the predicament he was in. At which point he would most likely make his presence known. But in the meantime, the kid had to get to the farm first, and that was what concerned Gio.

Trying not to drive like a maniac, Gio slowed as he reached the turning to Muddypuddle Lane and scanned the hedgerows and fields as he drove up the track. It was too much to hope that he would spot the child, but he looked anyway.

Dulcie was already waiting for him as he pulled into the yard. She must have heard the car, and her expression was hopeful when she saw who it was.

'I've not got any news,' he said as soon as he exited his vehicle, and her face crumpled.

She swiped at her tears and nodded when he asked if he could have a look around.

'Do you mind if I come with you?' she asked. 'Otto and I have checked everywhere. Twice. But Sammy's not very big and if he's here he could be hiding anywhere.' She bit her lip. 'Petra is checking the stables and her outbuildings, just in case. Do you think he has made it to Picklewick yet?'

'He may have. It's a two-hour journey by car, but more like three-and-three-quarters door to door by public transport. But then again he might not, especially when we don't know the time he left home. There's roughly a three-to-four-hour window.'

'Oh, god...' Dulcie's hand flew to her mouth. 'Poor little guy.'

'He'll be fine,' Gio said, despite knowing it was foolish to make reassurances. Resorting to a more professional tone, he added, 'The police will do their best to find him.' He clapped his hands together. 'Right, let's search the farm again, because it wouldn't surprise me if he's already here and keeping out of sight.'

An hour later, with the farm, the stables and the surrounding area thoroughly searched with the help of Otto, Nathan,

Megan and everyone at the stables, Gio admitted defeat. The lad was not here, and with the night closing in soon, he was becoming increasingly concerned.

The local force had turned up to speak to Dulcie, but his colleagues had been happy enough to let him continue searching the farm while they pursued other avenues. They had informed him that CCTV had shown Sammy boarding the four-fifty-five train at Birmingham New Street, and alighting at Thornbury station nearly two hours later. Which meant that Sammy should have been here by now...

Where the hell could he be?

Officers were checking with the bus company, and Gio was thankful that buses also carried CCTV. They would find him. He was sure of it.

It was just a matter of when.

'I'm going to walk into Picklewick across the fields,' he said. 'Maybe I can intercept him.' Assuming Sammy had arrived in Picklewick, that is. Gio hadn't received any updates for about an hour, so he was guessing that the police were still checking with the bus company. 'You stay at the farm,' he said to Dulcie, sensing that she was about to suggest she go with him. 'Nikki should be here any minute.'

He was desperate to see her, but finding Sammy took priority over his need to scoop her into his arms and tell her everything would be alright. Because, at this point, he couldn't honestly be sure it would be.

He was still hopeful of a positive outcome, though – Sammy was a bright lad with a sensible head on his shoulders, and Gio was convinced he was okay. Physically, at least. Sammy's emotional well-being was another matter entirely, and Gio's heart went out to the boy as he thought of how desperate the child must have felt in order to resort to running away to avoid returning to school on Monday.

With determination, he strode towards the row of holiday cottages belonging to the stables, heading for the public footpath which led across the fields to the edge of the village. The cottages had already been checked, whilst trying not to disturb the occupants too much. Two of them were currently rented out, although only the guests in one of them had been at home, and Petra had reluctantly gone inside the other for a quick look-see whilst they were out. Gio had entered the unoccupied third one with Petra, but there had been no sign of the boy.

As Gio hurried past, he saw two vehicles in the tiny car park and assumed that both sets of holidaymakers were now in residence. He debated whether to check with them again, but the cottages were only two-bed affairs, so the likelihood of a twelve-year-old boy hiding within their walls without the occupants noticing was slim to non-existent, so he decided not to bother and hurried past.

The grass in the fields was long, the golden stems teased by the breeze and creating waves of ripples. Gio narrowed his eyes at the movement. Sammy could be hunkered down in the grass and Gio would never see him, the constant sway of the stalks with their feathery seedheads, combined with the encroaching twilight, would serve to hide him from view.

Abruptly, Gio halted.

A nagging thought tugged at the back of his mind, and he glanced over his shoulder at the stables.

Something wasn't quite right, but he didn't know what...

Ah! Yes, he did.

He inhaled slowly, letting the memory of what he had just seen percolate through his mind. Had he imagined the twitch of a curtain at the upstairs window of the unoccupied holiday cottage? And if he hadn't imagined it, might it have been caused by the same breeze that whispered through the grass of the field he was standing in?

Probably.

It wouldn't hurt to double check, though.

And he had a hunch that there was more to this than a wind-blown curtain.

He took out his phone and dialled the number for the stables. Petra's husband, Harry, answered.

When Gio told him what he wanted him to do, Harry immediately agreed.

'Wait until you see me coming up the path,' Gio instructed. 'You can go in the front door, and I'll stake out the back. I probably imagined it, but if I haven't and Sammy **is** in there, I don't want to frighten him and risk him running out the back.'

'Gotcha,' Harry said.

Gio began walking back the way he'd come, praying he was right, hoping he wasn't wasting valuable time on a wild goose chase. If he remembered rightly, when he had searched the cottage with Petra, both the upstairs windows had been open, so it was fair to assume that a through breeze might have caused the curtains to move.

But at the same time, he knew in his gut that he was right.

Or was it just wishful thinking?

As he approached the row of cottages, he saw Harry hovering on the other side of the small car park, keeping out of sight of the cottage's windows, and Gio pointed to indicate he was heading around the back.

Holding up a hand, he mouthed, 'Five,' hoping Harry would give him enough time to get into position.

Gio didn't think Sammy would exit the building the same way he had entered it, which, if his hunch was correct, would have been by shimmying up the drainpipe and crawling in through the open bedroom window. Gio had noticed a key in the lock of the patio door, so he fully expected Sammy to leave in a more conventional manner – assuming that he **was** inside, of course.

He had only just reached the private garden at the back of the cottage and was forcing his way through the shrubbery, when Gio heard Harry shout, 'Sammy! Wait up!' and he knew he was right. Adrenaline shot through him as he scrambled to reach the door.

The boy ran to the patio doors, a panicked expression on his pale face, wrestling with the key, and had unlocked it before he noticed Gio.

Then his body sagged and his face crumpled.

Gio rushed over and grabbed hold of him, pulling him into his embrace, and as Sammy's body shuddered with deep sobs, Gio squeezed him tighter.

'I've got you,' he muttered, 'You're safe now. Everything's going to be okay.'

Releasing his grip for a second, Gio hooked his phone out of his jeans pocket, unlocking the screen with his thumb, then he tossed it to Harry, who looked as relieved as Gio felt.

'Call his mum,' Gio instructed, not wanting Nikki to have to wait another second longer to know that her son was safe. 'Tell her we'll be at the farm in five minutes.'

He turned his attention back to Sammy, who was sobbing uncontrollably. 'It's okay,' he repeated. 'Everything's going to be okay.'

'It's not!' Sammy wailed. 'Mum is going to be so mad.'

'She probably will,' Gio agreed. 'But that's only because she has been so worried about you. I'll tell you what else she'll be – relieved that you're safe. She loves you very, very much, you know.'

'I know.' Sammy's sobs were subsiding into sniffles, and Gio sensed it was time to step back to give the boy some space.

He slung an arm around his shoulders and gave him a sideways hug instead. 'Let's go see your Mum, shall we?'

Sammy nodded, but they hadn't made it as far as the lane when Nikki came tearing down it, running as though she was being chased by the devil himself.

'Sammy!' she shrieked, her face streaked with tears, and she barrelled into them, almost knocking her son off his feet as she grabbed hold of him.

Gio stood aside, his heart melting at the sight of her.

He should let his colleagues know that the boy had been found, but he stole a few seconds to drink her in.

Finally, though, he had to look away, and he used the excuse of the need to phone the station as he headed towards the farm and his car. Harry wordlessly gave him his phone back, clapping him on the shoulder as he passed and giving him a knowing look.

Then, with his heart breaking all over again, Gio walked away from the love of his life.

'I honestly don't know what to do,' Nikki said to Dulcie, that same evening. It was getting late, and Nikki was exhausted but too strung up to think about going to bed.

She was wearing borrowed pyjamas, having been persuaded that staying the night at the farm was more sensible than driving back to Birmingham.

Once all the furore had died down and phone calls to the police, Nikki's mum, Maisie, and Sammy's friends had been made, Otto, bless him, had rustled up a meal for everyone, although both she and Sammy had only picked at it, then she had put Sammy to bed, staying with him until he'd fallen asleep.

Even then she had been reluctant to take her eyes off him in case he ran away again, despite him promising he wouldn't. She believed him, but...

'Is it Sammy you don't know what to do about, or is it Gio?' Dulcie asked. 'More wine?'

'No, thanks. One glass is enough. I want to keep a clear head.' She wrinkled her nose. 'Both?'

'I thought so.'

'I have decided to give up work and teach Sammy at home,' Nikki said.

Her son and his abject misery were of more immediate concern than her love life, although she couldn't help wondering why Gio had dashed off so fast. He hadn't given her a chance to thank him, and when she had tried to call him later, it had gone straight to answerphone. She had thought about sending him a message, but she wanted to thank him in person. If he hadn't realised that Sammy was hiding out in one of Petra's holiday lets...

Nikki shuddered. Sammy would have been safe enough there, but she wouldn't have known that, and it was the not-knowing that had almost driven her mad. When Harry had called to tell her that Sammy had been found and he was okay, the relief that had swept through her had almost floored her.

Nikki never, ever wanted to go through anything like that again.

Which brought her back to the reason Sammy had run away in the first place, and whether there was anything she could have done to prevent it.

Her guilt was crippling, and tears welled, spilling over to trickle down her face. With an angry hand, Nikki brushed them away.

'It's my fault,' she said. 'I'm his mother, I should have taken him out of school a long time ago.'

'Hindsight is wonderful,' Dulcie said, scooting across the sofa to put her arm around her. 'You did what you thought was right.'

'But it **wasn't** right.' Nikki sniffed loudly. 'I'm going to ask Mum if we can move in with her.'

'What about your house?'

'I'll rent it out. It will give me some income. And maybe I can find some bar work in the evenings.'

Dulcie picked up her wine, her brow furrowed. 'You'll hate it.'

'Which bit?' Nikki asked dryly, dabbing at her eyes with a tissue.

'All of it – apart from spending more time with Sammy, of course. You'll hate living at home again after having your own place for so many years.' Dulcie shuddered. 'Then there's Maisie – she'll drive you nuts. Talk about having her head in the clouds. Did you know that

Mum still does all her laundry and cleans up after her?'

'I won't be doing any of that!' Nikki retorted. 'Maisie needs to grow up.'

'See, it's already getting you riled just thinking about it.'

'I know.'

'You're not going to like bar work, either,' Dulcie pointed out.

'If Maisie can do it, so can I!'

'I'm not saying you can't do it, I'm saying you won't like it. I know you – you like to be in bed by ten.'

'It's way past ten now, and I'm still up,' Nikki pointed out.

Dulcie arched an eyebrow.

'Yeah, okay, you're right,' Nikki conceded. 'I am usually in bed by ten. I'll just have to get used to staying up later, won't I?'

'What about your job? You love teaching.'

'I'll probably go back to it again at some point.'

'When Sammy is sixteen? Eighteen? When?'

'What's your point, Dulcie? I don't see I have any other option.'

Dulcie grinned at her. '**I** do. You can live here.'

Nikki stared at her. 'You mean...move in with **you**?'

'Yep.'

'But why? It's a lovely offer and thank you, but it doesn't change anything. I'll still have to rent my house out, and there are far fewer jobs up for grabs in Picklewick than there are in Birmingham.'

Dulcie was shaking her head and laughing. 'Look at the bigger picture,' she urged. 'If you and Sammy move into the farm, you can still rent your house out, but...' She paused, her grin turning into a beaming smile. 'You don't have to home educate Sammy; he can go to the school in Thornbury, and – here's the best bit – you can still teach. I don't know much about your job, but I'm guessing that the need for supply teachers isn't limited to Birmingham. And you know how much Sammy loves being here.'

Nikki knew, alright – after all, this was where he had escaped to when he'd thought he would have to return to school. To give herself time to think and to process what Dulcie had said, Nikki joked, 'You just want me to move in because of my unrivalled skills with a paintbrush.'

'That, too. You've got to admit it though, it's a brilliant idea.'

'What about Otto?' Won't us being here cramp your style?'

'Not at all. He'll understand. Anyway, I'm guessing you won't want to live with your little sister forever. You are eventually going to want to get a place of your own in Picklewick. But until then, this is the ideal solution.'

Nikki had to admit that it certainly seemed like it. As Dulcie had pointed out, Sammy would have a fresh start in a new school, and she could carry on with her supply teaching. Sammy would love living at the farm, and even if she did find somewhere of their own to live in the fullness of time, he could still pop to the farm whenever he wanted.

There was one fly in this rather appealing ointment though, and that was Gio.

How would he feel about her moving to Picklewick?

Would he be happy to have her nearby and for them to resume their relationship? Or had it been just a summer love, ripped at the seams by her return to Birmingham and never to be stitched together again?

There was only one way to find out.

Nikki sat in her car, the engine still running. Now that she was here, she wasn't convinced that turning up at Gio's house at this time of night was such a good idea after all. It was incredibly late, and he mightn't even be in as there weren't any lights on. And if he was, he might not want to see her.

Maybe she should come back in the morning, but this time she would call ahead first.

She tapped her fingers on the steering wheel, torn. If she left now, she suspected she wouldn't have the courage to return. And if she didn't speak to him and ask how he would feel about her coming to Picklewick to live, then she would have to resort to plan B and move in with her mum, because visiting Picklewick would be bad enough — she couldn't even begin to imagine living here and not being with him. Her heart simply wouldn't be able to take it.

What should she do?

In some ways she wished Dulcie had never suggested it, then she wouldn't be in such a quandary. But her sister's idea was a good one – a brilliant one, even – because in one fell swoop moving to Picklewick would solve all her and Sammy's problems.

But would it work?

That depended on Gio.

Which brought her back to the reason she was sitting in her car outside his house, trying to pluck up the courage to knock on his door.

Gio solved the problem for her when he tapped on the passenger window, making her shriek and almost jump out of her skin.

Putting a hand to her chest and her frantically beating heart, she wound the window down. 'Hi.'

'Hi, you.' His voice was soft, his expression thoughtful.

She said, 'I came to thank you.'

'It's late,' he pointed out.

'Yet, here I am.'

'Here you are,' he repeated slowly.

It was now or never, she decided, her courage almost failing her as she blurted the words. 'Can I come in?'

'Of course.' He waited for her to get out of the car and his eyebrows shot up when he saw she was wearing PJs. 'Planning on staying the night?' he joked, then winced. 'Sorry, I didn't mean that to sound the way it did.'

Seeing him again, Nikki would like nothing better than to stay the night. She would like to stay **every** night, not just one.

She followed him inside, hesitating when she got as far as the end of the hall. Then she took a deep breath and walked into the kitchen. 'I'm sorry it's so late. I had to speak to you and you didn't answer your phone.'

'I went for a run, to clear my head.'

She realised he was wearing running shorts and trainers. 'Just got back?'

'Uh-huh. Would you like a drink?'

'Not for me, thanks.' She watched him pour himself a glass of water, her eyes on his throat as he drank it down. 'I came to thank you for finding Sammy,' she repeated. 'And to ask you a question.'

'You don't need to thank me. It was sheer luck that I noticed the curtain moving. I'm just glad he's okay.'

'He's fine. For now. Not so sure how fine he'll be when I take him home. Actually, that's why I'm here. I...er...wondered how you would feel if I moved here. Me and Sammy. Into the farm. With Dulcie,' she stuttered.

Gio didn't answer and his expression didn't give anything away, so she hastily explained, 'I've decided not to send him back to school. I was planning on moving back in with my mum and home educating him. But Dulcie suggested that I live with her instead. For the time being, at least. Sammy loves it here, and he could go to the school in Thornbury, and—'

'What about **you**?' Gio leapt in.

'I love it here, too. It's a brilliant idea, but...'

'But...?'

'God, this is awkward.' She raised her eyes to the ceiling and took a steadying breath, before coming to rest on him again.

'I get it,' he said, nodding slowly. 'It won't be a problem. I don't expect us to take up where we left off.' He didn't meet her gaze.

She swallowed. This was exactly what she feared he might say. He might have told her he loved her, but that was when there was no prospect of them being together. The reality of her moving to Picklewick was an altogether different thing.

Plan B it was, then. She said, 'Look, forget it. It was a daft idea. Sorry.'

'I think it's a great idea,' he said. 'Don't let my love for you prevent you from doing what's best for you and Sammy.'

Nikki froze. 'What did you say?'

'It's a great idea?'

'After that.' She made a winding-on motion with her hand.

Gio pulled a face. 'I said, don't let my love for you stop you. Don't worry, I'll stay well clear. I went into this with my eyes wide open: just because you're moving to Picklewick, doesn't mean I'll assume we are going to be a couple.'

Nikki thought her heart was going to burst out of her chest. Happiness washed over her as her face crumpled. Don't cry, she told herself.

Then she immediately burst into tears.

Gio gathered her to him. 'Shhh,' he murmured. 'It's alright, everything is alright. He's safe now.'

'I'm not crying because of Sammy,' she wept. 'I'm crying because you love me. I thought you didn't want me anymore, that this was just a summer romance to you.'

'It was never just a summer romance. I love you with all my heart, and I would like nothing more than for us to be together – a proper couple.'

Nikki lifted her head, sniffling back tears. 'How proper?'

He was smiling at her, love in his eyes. 'Proper enough that I want to be with you all day, every day. I know that isn't possible, but...'

'You'll be able to see as much of me as you want when I move to the farm.'

'It's not enough,' he insisted. 'I want **more**. I want you to come live with **me**.' He suddenly looked worried. 'Or am I going too fast for you?'

Nikki was astounded. **Move in with Gio...?**

Her heart almost stopped at the enormity of it. But her first instinct was to say yes. So that was what she did.

'I'd love that, too,' she said. 'I'll have to discuss it with Sammy, though.'

'Of course you will. He has got to be on board with it, and if he isn't, I'll have to try harder to win him round. I love you, Nikki, and I never want to let you go.'

And he didn't, not for a very long time indeed.

'Where do you want this?'

Nikki was standing in Gio's bedroom (her bedroom now, too) and she glanced around to see Gio nodding his head at the box he was holding. 'Um, I'm not sure what's in it.' She had packed up the house in Birmingham in such a hurry, that she wasn't quite sure what she had shoved into which box. 'Aw, stuff it! Stick it in the shed. I'll sort it out when I can find the time.'

Gio grinned at her, walking away with the box, leaving Nikki to finish dragging clothes out of a suitcase and hastily shove them on hangars in the wardrobe.

She disliked mess and wanted to find a place for as many things as she could before the day was out, knowing that tomorrow was going to be busy. She had to take Sammy to buy his new school uniform (thankfully the trousers and shoes she had purchased for him at the end of the summer were suitable) and she had an interview with a supply agency afterwards. Although...she was secretly hoping to land herself a permanent job, and she had already begun looking.

Thinking about Sammy had her praying he was behaving himself. It had been easier to drop him at the stables whilst she got on with the unpacking, rather than trip over him every five minutes, because he was as bubbly as a bottle of fizz with the cork out at being in Picklewick. His happiness was a delight to behold.

Gio reappeared, having deposited the box in the shed along with the rest of the bits and pieces she had yet to find a home for.

Most of her furniture was in one of the barns on the farm. She had briefly considered putting everything into storage, but Dulcie had told her not to be so silly and had offered her the use of the redundant sheep shed for the duration. Her furniture was now stacked neatly under several layers of tarpaulin, until she decided what to do with it.

After all, Gio had plenty of furniture of his own and his house didn't need an additional sofa or a second washing machine – although it very definitely did need a woman's touch, and she was the woman to provide it.

'Come here,' he said, holding his arms open for her to step into his embrace. 'No regrets?'

'None, whatsoever,' her reply was emphatic. 'Mind you, I might change my mind if you leave dirty socks on the floor or I have to nag you to take the bins out,' she teased.

'I'm completely house trained,' he objected with a laugh. 'But I know someone who isn't.'

Nikki gasped. 'Sammy is a pre-teen! He's not supposed to be house trained. It says so in the 'How to be a Teenager' manual.'

'I wasn't referring to Sammy.'

'Then who? Not me, I hope?'

'Come downstairs, I've got something to show you.' He grabbed her hand and towed her out of the bedroom, across the landing and down the stairs. 'Actually, it's not some**thing**, it's some**one**.' He led her into the kitchen. 'Meet Tara. She's an eleven-week-old border collie, and she's Sammy's housewarming present. Do you think he'll like her?'

'Are you kidding!' Nikki squealed, dropping to her knees to pick up the bewildered pup. 'He'll adore her!'

'I did think about getting him a chicken, but you can't take a chicken for a walk or play ball with it, and I remembered him saying how much he wanted a dog. I hope you don't mind,' Gio added worriedly.

'Mind? Of course I don't mind! That is such a nice thing to do.' She cuddled the tiny dog to her chest, sniffing its puppy smell and stroking the fluffy fur. Tara licked her hand, squirming in her arms as she tried to reach Nikki's face.

Gently Nikki returned the puppy to its basket, straightened up and turned to face Gio.

'Thank you. Have I told you how much I love you?' she said, offering her mouth to him.

It was only meant to be a quick kiss, but as always it turned into something much longer and far more satisfying, and when she reluctantly extricated herself because the pup was whining and making a fuss, Gio's face was so woebegone that she had to laugh.

'Never mind,' she said. 'There's always later, and this time I won't have to sneak out in the early hours of the morning. I still can't believe you asked me to move in with you.'

'I still can't believe you said yes,' he countered. 'I would have put hard cash on you saying it was too soon.'

'Other people might think that, but I don't,' she said, remembering the conversation she'd had with her mum, and the one she'd had with Dulcie. But Sammy had thought it was a wonderful idea once he realised that he could pop to the farm and the stables anytime he wanted, and the way he had taken to Gio warmed her heart.

And now Gio had bought him a puppy...

The very same puppy who was pawing at her leg right now. 'I think this little one wants some attention,' she said. 'You'll have to wait.'

'I don't mind,' Gio said, his eyes so full of love it made her heart ache with the beauty of it. 'We have all the time in the world.'

He was right – they did – but Nikki didn't want to waste a second of it.

She had come to the farm on Muddypuddle Lane to escape, but she could never have anticipated being caught by the intense and unequivocal love she felt for Gio. And now that she had, she intended to relish every moment. The puppy would be fine on its own for a short while – Nikki wanted to show her wonderful man just how much she loved him!

There are loads more large print books in the Muddypuddle Lane series. Available at all good book stores, or ask your local library.

About Etti

Etti Summers is the author of wonderfully romantic fiction with happy ever afters guaranteed.

She is also a wife, a mum, a pink gin enthusiast, a veggie grower and a keen reader.

Printed in Great Britain
by Amazon